A Thug's Betrayal   Sativa Outlaw

A Thug's Betrayal

by

Sativa Outlaw

Text **LEOSULLIVAN** to 22828 to join our mailing list!

To submit a manuscript for our review, email us at <u>leosullivanpresents@gmail.com</u>

© 2015

Published by Leo Sullivan Presents

www.leolsullivan.com

CHAPTER 1

It was their senior year, and Leroy couldn't wait for that damn bell to ring. Looking up at the clock, he didn't understand why time chose to creep on the last day. He loved his last two years at Lakeview High School. Leaving with a diploma, a fine ass girlfriend, and their one-year-old son, he felt he was winning. Leroy felt a light tap on his shoulder; turning around, he saw Lisa smiling as she leaned up, kissing him. "Can you believe it, baby? We're high school graduates!" She bit his lip as the teacher yelled for them to settle down.

He gazed around the room, wondering where all his soon to be former classmates would be in five years. He wanted to be married with his own business and hopefully, more kids. Ten more minutes and it seemed as if someone had frozen the clock; Mr. Hampton scribbled brainstorming activities on the board to try to keep busy. "You guys can waste time by writing your favorite foods."

Leroy immediately wrote down pizza, pizza burgers, and burgers. Laughing at himself, he turned around and noticed Lisa had written pizza for number one. Smiling, he stood up, getting ready for the bell.

Making the clock noise with his mouth, Leroy held Lisa's hand as she leaned her juicy ass against his desk. She tapped her feet anxiously, as her titties bounced. Her light brown skin made her blonde hair stand out as she bit her bottom lip. Lisa mouthed the numbers as she counted down the seconds until the bell rang. Before the ding, Lisa's ex-boyfriend, Jamal, brushed past them, bumping into Leroy, who immediately went after him. Lisa grabbed for his arm and he jerked away, following her ex outside.

"Muhfucka, you got a prollem wid me?" Leroy walked up on Jamal, who had a pissed off look on his face.

Jamal grabbed his waist, turning his head side to side. "Muhfucka do you got a prollem wid me?"

Leroy sees the gun and shakes his head. "Next time, bitch."

Jamal smirks, "Indeed bitch." Jamal disappeared around the corner of the school, as Leroy headed to his '98 Chevy Caprice, and unlocked his glove compartment. Grabbing his 9mm, he decided to show Jamal exactly who the bitch was. Leroy could see Lisa standing in the door, begging him to come to her. She didn't realize how done he was with her ex's shit, and the only way to end it was with a bullet. He walked around the corner, hiding behind the big bush the class painted a year ago. Leroy could see Jamal talking to some white guy in a black hoodie. The whole thing looked suspicious as fuck, and then the white guy smacked Jamal across the face with a gun. Leroy saw Jamal hit the pavement hard as the white guy began to rummage through Jamal's pockets.

Quickly making up his mind, Leroy cocked his gun, easing his way over to the hooded man, and aiming the barrel at the back of his head. "Yo bitch ass got two seconds to drop 'ery fuckin thang and ease yo ass against that wall." Leroy could see that Jamal's face was busted up and he wasn't fully conscious.

The guy in the hoodie stood up slowly, and Leroy cracked him on the top of the head with the butt of the gun. By this time, Jamal began to come to as Leroy threw him the bundle of cash and the drugs. Jamal looked confused, rubbing the back of his head, and kicking the hooded guy in the stomach. Nodding at Leroy to let him know he was grateful, he also opened the bundle of cash and handed him six, crisp, hundred-dollar bills. Leroy looked at him, shoving the money in his pocket.

"Jus' 'cause you a bitch don't mean you should go out like one," Jamal laughed as he and Leroy made their way back to the front of the building.

Leroy could see Lisa's blonde braids sway in the wind as she paced back and forth worried about her man. "Baby, calm yo thick ass down," he called out to her.

Turning around her eyes lit up; she thought for a moment that she had lost him. "Don't yo light skin ass ever scare me like that again." She wrapped her arms around his neck, as he lifted her off her feet. Standing at 5'11, he loved that she was only 4'9; he could do what he wanted with her. He hugged her tight, kissing her neck as Jamal stood there and watched them with a disgusted face.

"Yo ass ain't gettin rid of me that easy."

Jamal waited for him to put her down and shook his hand. "Good lookin' on that shit, fam, can't trust them white fiend muhfuckas."

"Shit, I'd want a nigga to look out fa me, and dem hunnids was enough thanks." They looked at each other as if they had just met, and Jamal figured he wasn't as bad as he thought.

Leroy was walking away toward his vehicle; Jamal thought for a second and called out to him. "Aye Lee, nigga, catch me tomorrow after graduation." All Leroy could do was shake his head up and down; he still didn't trust Jamal, but he was straight as long as he got paid.

CHAPTER 2

"Aye baby, you seen my blue and white J's?" Leroy poked his head into their one-year-old son's bedroom. Lisa held her son's legs in the air, rubbing him down with baby lotion.

"Hold still, LJ; baby, look under the bed on my side." Lisa was only seventeen with a one-year-old, but she loved her little family, and she still was graduating; she was happy. She and Leroy had been together two years; she had spent her middle school years with Jamal, who now was a crazed-minded thug.

"Good lookin' bae." He ran up behind her, kissing her neck softly as she giggled, putting on LJ's pull-up.

"You know I gotchu, baby."

He ran and grabbed his good luck sneakers and wrapped his and Lisa's cap and gown around his shoulders. "Mami, I'm finna put these in the car, then I'll help with bad ass."

"Thanks bae." They weren't perfect, but it worked and they loved each other. Besides, as Beyoncé said, who wants that perfect love story anyway?

Leroy laid their gowns on the seat and adjusted LJ's car seat. By the time he made it back inside, Lisa had already gotten LJ dressed, and was brushing his curly black hair. His son had his eyes, and his mother's skin, bound to be a heartbreaker. "You packed his diaper bag, ma?" Leroy asked as he searched the room for his son's favorite toy, a Woody doll from *Toy Story*. They had been forced to watch that movie over a hundred times, but it was all worth it for his baby boy.

"Umm, shit yeah, baby, erything except his bibs and toy." Lisa kissed her son's well-greased face and picked him up from the beige changing table Leroy built for her. "Okay baby erything ready to drop him off at Mama Pearl's house." Mama Pearl was Lisa's grandma; she was old, but acted as if she was twenty-one. She loved watching LJ and even offered to keep him while they celebrated finishing high school. Leroy leaned down, kissing Lisa very slow, as she held his shirt, pulling him closer.

"We love you, daddy." Lisa smiled at him, staring into his eyes as he took LJ.

"Daddy love y'all just as much, baby."

Strapping LJ into his car seat, Leroy heard his phone buzz. He figured everyone would be at the stadium, calling him. Grabbing his phone from his back pocket, he saw an unknown number's text saying, "Don't forget our meeting." He immediately knew whom it was from, and he kept it from Lisa. It was hard explaining why he'd helped Jamal the first time; he knew she wasn't going to be happy knowing they were meeting up. "Ready mami?" He leaned over, biting her cheek softly.

"Damn skippy, baby." She smiled as Leroy headed down four blocks to drop LJ off at Mama Pearl's house. He pulled up in front of the gate of the brick house, helping Lisa grab LJ's things. They could see Mama Pearl sitting in her bench swing on her porch; she waved as they walked towards her. She hugged Lisa tight, kissing her cheek and leaving a big red lipstick mark.

"I'm so proud of y'all, me and LJ gon' be there soon, y'all finish getting ready." Leroy leaned closer, hugging the old woman; she was always there when they needed her. They both kissed their son, as they hopped in the car, making their way to the high school.

"Bae, can you believe it? Next month, no more waking up seeing teachers' faces; we can lay up and watch cartoons all day." Lisa smiled at the vision of her boyfriend's words in her head.

"Not all day, baby." She rubbed his leg.

"Gotta kill the dream don't you?"

They pulled into a parking spot, seeing Jamal standing out front, waiting for them. "Sup, old muhfuckas." He threw both his hands up in the air, waving them over. Lisa screwed up her face; she still didn't trust him, but she was the Bonnie to Leroy's Clyde. Where he went, she went; no questions asked.

"Sup nigga, ready to become a man?" Jamal and Leroy locked hands and they shoulder hugged.

Jamal slapped Leroy on the back. "Nigga, I became a man when me and yo mama had you." They both laughed, as Leroy playfully pushed him.

"Yeah, whatever nigga; me and yo moms been talking; we decided it's time fa yo ass to move out."

The three of them laughed, heading into the gym to get changed into their cap and gowns. As Jamal headed into the boys' locker room, Leroy followed behind Lisa .

"I'll see you when I'm done, daddy." She jumped into his arms, kissing him slow and hard as he pressed her back up against the wall.

"Baby, I'on think I can wait until afterwards." He slid his tongue down her neck, tasting her Pure Paradise Bath & Body Works perfume. She wrapped her legs around his waist, nibbling on his ear, feeling him press his hard dick up against her warm mound.

"Baby, we don't have long, gotta get ready," Lisa whispered in between moans. Leroy rubbed his hands down her chest slowly; lifting up her skirt, he put her legs up on his shoulders. Lisa gasped as he gripped her waist, moving her thong to the side with his tongue; he softly kissed her clit as her legs quivered. Lisa rubbed the back of his waved head, rolling her hips slowly against his warm tongue. She leaned her head back against the wall as he sucked her throbbing clit into his mouth. Feeling her arch her back, Leroy slid his wet tongue deep inside of her, as Lisa screamed, "Baby, I love you."

CHAPTER 3

Lisa couldn't keep a huge smile from spreading across her face; she had her man, her beautiful son, and now her diploma. She was the first in her family to graduate, and she was more proud of herself than anyone else was. Hearing her name, she strutted in her heels and crimson red skirt onto the stage, shaking hands and waving as her friends and family screamed her name.

She looked into the crowd and a tear fell from her face; she could see her son waving, saying, "Go Mommy." Besides him being born, today was the proudest moment of her life. Lisa ran over to LJ, grabbing him from Mama Pearl's arms as she kissed Lisa's forehead.

"Mama loves you, baby; I do this for you." Lisa kissed LJ as they waited for Leroy to walk the stage. Lisa had to take her heels off, at the sound of Leroy's name; she jumped up and down so hard that LJ dropped Woody. "Yeaah, goooo baaaaaby," she yelled loudly, as LJ waved at his daddy. Leroy looked at her and winked, flashing his sexy ass smile, and adjusting his glasses. She bit her lip; he made her knees weak and she couldn't wait until this was over, because she had plans for that body of his.

Leroy ran over, pulling Lisa and LJ into his arms smiling; he would do right by his little family, no matter what the cost.

Jamal and Leroy decided to throw a small get together at the Red Diamond Strip Club; they deserved ass in their face. "The fuck you mean Lisa comin', nigga?" Jamal leaned back in the sofa chair in Leroy's living room, rolling a blunt of Master Kush.

"Look nigga, she asked and hey, that's bae. If we can rub a booty together, I'm winning." He rubbed his hands together, grinning as Lisa came out of LJ's room, putting her finger to her lip.

"Damn, I'm like a few inches away muhfuckas, I can hear; bet not wake my son up wit' that shit." She grabbed the blunt from Jamal's hands and lit it. "Fuckin' right I'm going nigga, fuck yo feelings." Taking a long drag from the blunt, she blows the smoke in his direction, smiling. "Y'all muhfuckas need to learn how to get along, damn. Mama Pearl gon' be here soon and we can get drunk."

Jamal tipped his red cup. "You mean drunker." Leroy took the blunt from Lisa's hand, sitting next to her as they waited for her granny to arrive. "Aye Lee, 'member that white boy tried to pop me?" Leroy took a hit from the blunt, shaking his head up and down. Jamal continued on, "I know where ol' boy be at, he just keep shit lying round." Before Jamal could tell him more,

Mama Pearl walked in, as Lisa grabbed the blunt, putting it out.

"Y'all got it stinking in here, betta save Mama some." Lisa laughed, handing her the rest of the blunt; she sniffed it, wrinkling up her face. "Pooh stank real good for Mama." They all laughed as they gave her another hug, telling her there were food and snacks in their fridge and room.

"A'ight Mama thanks again." Leroy kissed her cheek.

"We won't stay out too late; I promise, Ma," Lisa smiled, hugging her grandmother.

"Bet not, or we gon' come where the party at." They laughed, knowing that she was dead ass serious. That night, they decided to let Jamal drive, since he was treating them that night. Leroy and Lisa matched in their white and blue True Religion his and her shirts; he wore black Levis and she had on black jeggings. She wore her Timberland heels and he wore his black Timberlands. Jamal wore a black button up with all white Trues. His red Camaro rode very smooth; they smoked almost three more blunts before making their way to the club.

"Baaaby, I'ma get up on the pole, it say it's amateur night." Since Leroy was good and high, and being horny as hell, he agreed. He trusted her and knew she was coming home to him, so her bouncing her ass was no problem, but her clothes had better stay on. "I got some bills fa you baby, none bet not come off." She kissed his cheek, "I know bae... I know bae."

She checked her make up as Leroy brushed his waves; Jamal watched them in the rear view mirror. "Y'all ready or nah?" As they exited the car, they heard Rae Sremmurd and Nicki Minaj's "Throw Sum Mo" booming from the club. The line was long almost as the corner, but Jamal walked up to the bouncer, shook his hand and escorted them inside. Lisa remembered that being with Jamal; he always got whatever he wanted no matter what. Well, everything except her, that was. They made their way to the bar; Jamal asked the bartender for three bottles of Henny, one for each of them. Leroy cracked his, knocking it back, but Lisa sipped from hers, saving a little until later. After finishing two of the bottles, Jamal sat in the corner, receiving a lap dance from a stripper named Felicity. He buried his face into her huge white breasts; Leroy laid back, watching Desire bounce her ass as Lisa shoved ones in her G-string. Leroy rubbed her ass as Lisa smacked it; she pulled the stripper toward her and their faces lit up. Lisa pulled off her shirt and underneath was a tank top; Leroy licked his lips as Desire led her on stage. Lisa bent over grabbing her ankles; looking at Leroy over her shoulder, she rolled her hips very slowly to "Pornstar" by August Alsina. She grabbed the pole, and began spinning around, wrapping her legs around it, as Leroy stood up throwing bills on the stage.

He rubbed her thighs as she spread her legs, grinding against the stage, and Leroy grabbed his dick watching her. He grabbed her hand, helping her off the stage. He kissed her hard, pulling her into his arms and grabbing her ass with both hands. Lisa locked her arms around her man's neck, sucking on his ear; the liquor had hit them both hard. For a moment they had forgotten that they were there with Jamal, who dipped off toward the bar, watching them with a glare in his eye. He'd never realized how much Lisa had meant to him. Maybe it was the liquor or seeing her dance like that, but the hormones and rage fueled up inside of him, setting his body on fire. A part of him wanted her back and a part of him wanted to make this money, but maybe he could have it both ways. Walking over to Lisa and Leroy with a fake smile on his face, Jamal handed them some Cîroc shots. For now, he would play nice, but his empire wouldn't be complete without his queen by his side.

CHAPTER 4

A few weeks had passed and Leroy had gotten a job at a garage, fixing brakes. LJ's birthday was in two days and they wanted to get him the Toy Story bouncy house he kept asking for. To be a one-year-old, he was very demanding, but it was his world and he could have whatever he wanted. The garage paid okay, but he had to work overtime all that week and barely had time for Lisa. He made plans for them to have a little date night; he knew she needed that treatment. He texted her that he loved her and to kiss LJ and he would be home in a few hours. She texted him back a picture of LJ asleep and her in a t-shirt with nothing on underneath. He instantly got hard thinking about digging deep inside of her, but hearing a knock on the garage door brought him back to reality.

He walked to the front desk; Jamal was standing there, counting a wad of money. "Nigga, what's goody?" They shook hands as Jamal followed Leroy into the back office.

"Shit nigga been here all day, so ready to go." Jamal looked around the office; he noticed all the certificates for excellent service with Leroy's name on them. "Nigga,

I'on see how you can do it, working for somebody waitin' on a check; I needs my money on time." Slapping his hand, he laughed as Leroy rubbed his head.

"Shit nigga, jus' doin' what I gotta do."

Jamal sat in the chair opposite Leroy, taking a fat joint from his pocket. Leroy threw him a lighter, and Jamal lit it, blowing smoke rings. "I feel you, fam, and speaking of which, I got a proposition fa ya." Handing Leroy the joint, Jamal takes the wad from his pocket. "It's fa you, all of it, all you gotta do is help me with this job I gotta do."

Leroy grabbed the wad of money, looking confused and started to count it. "Nigga this bout three g's, type of fuckin job is it?"

Taking a long drag from the joint, Jamal smiles, "Crazy ass white boy, got a house fulla shit, all you gotta do is help me get what I want, and you get paid, and this just for doing it. You get more after we done."

Leroy rubbed his hands together thinking, looking at the money, which was more than needed for LJ's party. He knew Lisa would be pissed, so if he were going to do it, he would have to keep her from finding out. "Shit nigga in my position, I'm down, just gotta keep it low key; Lisa would trip the fuck out." They shook hands as Leroy shoved the wad of money in his locked desk drawer. Jamal told him he'd call him when it was time to do the job. After Jamal left, Leroy looked at the money one more time; he still didn't trust Jamal, but he would do anything for LJ.

The day finally arriving, Lisa woke up early to make LJ's favorite breakfast of eggs, waffles, round sausage, and a bunch of grapes. She poured him a huge glass of Sunny Delight, as Leroy went in his room to wake him up. Lisa turned on his favorite movie *Toy Story 2*; sitting Woody next to LJ's place on the couch. Lisa saw Leroy and LJ walking out of his room, LJ's hands over his eyes. "Okay Mommy, I not lookin'." Leroy smiled, walking behind him, tickling him as he walked to the kitchen of their small apartment. Counting backwards from five, Leroy told LJ he could lower his hands, his little mouth dropped open. "Oh wow this is soo coool." He grabbed his new Woody doll from the couch, shoving a waffle and grape into his mouth. Leroy grinned from ear to ear, and Lisa had never been so happy, seeing their baby that excited was the best thing ever. Leroy grabbed his son into his arms, "Jus' wait and see what Mommy and Daddy got fa you later lil man." He jumped up and down yelling, "Daaddy, what is it, what is it?" He kissed his son's head, grabbing one of his waffles.

"Gotta wait lil daddy, be patient, you gon' love it." He hugged his father and ran over, hugging his mother, then sat on the couch with his toy and breakfast watching his movie. Leroy and Lisa hugged each other tight, watching TV with their son.

By the end of the movie, for the tenth time, Leroy's phone began to ring. Lisa grabbed it; the caller ID read Mal. "Fuck he want, bae, we gotta start his party in two hours."

He took his phone, kissing her cheek. "Jus' gimme a few minutes, baby." Leroy stepped outside, answering his phone. "Sup nigga, you ready?" Leroy could hear the EL in the background.

"Yeah nigga, I'll be there in 'bout ten minutes, jus' be outside."

"Bet." Leroy hung up the phone, with Lisa staring at him as he came back inside.

"So the fuck is up?" she asked. He picked her up in his arms, kissing the wrinkle in her forehead. "Mami, calm down, and I promise I'll be back in time."

Lisa locked her arms tight around his neck. "Fuckin' betta be." She bit his lip, kissing him, as LJ lay asleep in front of the flat screen. Before heading to the corner to wait for Jamal, Leroy called the toy store, reserving the bouncy house for his son. "Yeah, I'll pay the extra for delivery and setup." Shoving his phone in his pocket, as the Chicago winds blew, he put his glasses in his coat as he saw Jamal walk up, with a duffle bag over his right shoulder. The two men shook hands, as they walked towards the suburbs of Chicago. Jamal checked his surroundings and handed Leroy a 9mm, which he tucked under his t-shirt. "So when we get there, he gon' be in the garage, erything I need is in the basement."

Turning the corner, Jamal let him know to keep the white boy busy, while he grabbed the shit. "And if the muhfucka try anything, body his ass."

Leroy thought hard about that, he ain't sign up to kill nobody, and hopefully it wouldn't come to that. "Nigga, let's jus' finish this shit, my son birthday today."

Jamal smiled, smacking his back, "Aww shit, I gotta get the lil nigga sum'." They made their way to the front of a brick house; the gate was high and black. The garage light was on, and they could hear loud rock music echoing from inside. Jamal motioned for Leroy to head toward the left and he;d take the right; they had to make sure he was alone. Leroy peeked into the garage window, seeing the boy in the same hoodie, sniffing coke from a glass mirror. He shakes his head, as Jamal heads inside; Leroy aims his gun at the boy's head, getting ready to shoot if he moved. Jamal tried the front door; it instantly opened, and he made his way to the basement and rummaged through all the boxes. He immediately found ten bricks of cocaine, and almost fifty thousand in cash. Trying not to get too excited, Jamal shoves the shit in the bag as fast as possible. He was almost done when he hears a gunshot. His eyes at the door, he cocks his gun, walking toward the garage slowly. He sees Leroy standing over the basehead. He was holding his leg yelling for help.

"Bitch, shut the fuck up." Jamal aims the gun at his head, pulling the trigger; his head bangs against the floor with a loud thud.

Leroy and Jamal took the city bus back to their side of town; stopping at Jamal's to divide the ends. "Damn nigga fuck you kill him fa?" Leroy asked as he counted his half of the money, watching Jamal stash the keys in a secret compartment under the floor.

"Shit, save his boss the trouble; muhfucka was dead when we robbed him anyway." Ignoring Jamal's rant, Leroy grabbed his coat making his way to the door. "Good lookin' my nigga gotta get home."

Jamal shook his hand. "Shit couldn't do it wit out ya bruh." As Leroy opened the door, Jamal yelled out, "I'ma let you know when we got anotha one." Leroy walked down the street, waiting for the bus to get to his baby's party. He didn't know how good he felt, making a hobby out of this; he wouldn't want his son doing it. However, in a way he felt that if he did it, LJ wouldn't have to worry about a thing.

He made it just in time; everyone had arrived, and Mama Pearl held LJ while Lisa poured juice for the kids. The bouncy house was fully blown up, and LJ was going to be first inside. Leroy ran up grabbing his son. He kissed Lisa. "I love you baby," he whispered to her as he took his son inside the bouncy house, helping other kids on. LJ jumped high, screaming and laughing. Leroy saw the smile on his face and on Lisa's and thought; they were whom he was doing all this wrong for.

CHAPTER 5

Lisa was searching Leroy's shoeboxes for one of LJ's toys. He wanted to be like his father so bad; he stored his important toys in boxes just as Leroy stores his things in them. She grabbed the box that held the shoes he wore to graduation, and she wondered why it was so heavy, just for shoes. She sat it on the bed; opening it, her jaw dropped. She saw a bunch of money and a silver 9mm; she was so mad she couldn't even scream. Leroy had gon' to drop LJ off at Mama's so they could have their date night. Now, it wasn't going to be anything nice or cordial when he stepped in the door.

She held the gun in her hand, as Leroy walked inside the apartment, calling out, "Baby, get yo ass ova here, big daddy home." He turned around and his face instantly turned red, he walked over to her and snatched the gun from her hand. "The fuck is wrong with you, dammit, have you lost yo fuckin mind?"

Lisa pushed him hard. "No muhfucka, I think you done lost yours, bringing a fuckin' gun in the house with our son, fuck were you thinking, he goes in yo boxes, Lee." She ran towards him, pushing him hard as he hit the wall. Rolling his eyes, Leroy didn't want to hit his woman, but he would be damned if she manhandled him like a bitch.

Leroy shoved the gun in a cookie jar on top of the fridge, dodging Lisa as she came after him again. "Baby, jus' gimme a fuckin' minute and I'll explain erything, I promise." He grabbed her wrist, pulling her close and kissing her cheek. She turned her head, snatching away from him, sitting on the arm of their sofa.

"Go 'head nigga, I'm listenin'." She crossed her arms, staring at him with an evil glare.

Leroy sighed and walked over to her, wrapping his arms around her small waist. "Been doin shit wid Mal, jus' lil jobs baby, nun serious."

She jerked around with tears in her eyes; she never wanted to be a dope boy's wife. All she wanted was Leroy and LJ. "So yo ass used some fuckin' drug money to pay for my son's fuckin' birthday party?" Leroy could see her temper flaring, her light brown skin almost turning beet red with anger. He tried to grab for her hand and she slapped his face. "Leave me the fuck alone Lee."

Leroy rubbed his face, walking after her as she sat on the edge of the bed, texting Mama Pearl to check on LJ. "Baby, I promise, I been careful, I ain't tryna leave you and my lil nigga. Whether a box or a cage, bae; I ain't goin' nowhere." He lifted her head, kissing her lips, softly stroking her cheek gently.

Lisa couldn't help but believe Leroy's words; she loved him and knew that he was doing it for them. In the back of her mind, she just didn't want him to end up like Jamal, obsessed with money and power. She wrapped her arms around his neck, pulling him down on top of her. Leroy knew he had more explaining to do, but right now, all the blood in his dick said no more talking. He pressed his body against Lisa's, as she wrapped her legs around his waist. He could feel her pussy thumping underneath him, as he pulled her shirt over her shoulders, sliding his hand down and removing her shorts. Lisa bit down on Leroy's shoulder, as he rubbed his finger gently over her swollen clit. Lisa didn't notice Leroy that had already removed his jogging pants and boxers, until he was pressing the head of his thick dick up against her wet hole. Leroy grabbed the headboard, as Lisa locked her arms around his neck; they both seemed to float from their bodies. She could feel him pushing every inch as deep as he could go; all Lisa could do was scream as she gripped his dick tight, rolling her hips. "Baby, I love you, just don't leave me." Lisa could feel Leroy's dick pulsating inside of her as he wrapped his arms around her waist pushing even deeper.

"Fuck baby… told yo ass I ain't eva goin' nowhere."

Digging her nails into his back, Lisa pulled Leroy closer, feeling him pressing up against her G-spot. "Damn baby, you gon' cum on daddy dick?" Lisa laid her head on Leroy's shoulder, grinding her pussy harder against his dick as her body quivered. Leroy shoved deeper, making his balls slap against her with every thrust as Lisa screamed. Leroy could feel himself bust deep inside of her, as her warm cream covered his shaft. Leroy kissed her forehead gently, hugging her close. "Baby, I love yo feisty ass you ain't got shit to worry 'bout." She again felt comfort from his words; he had never lied to her before.

"Shit baby, that's all I needed to hear." Lisa kissed his lips softly, as he lay on his back holding her close and tight, they fell asleep in each other's arms. Sweet dreams of a big house, a dog, a daughter, and his wife had Leroy thinking he could stay in dreamland for a while, and not have a care in the world. His phone beeping from text messages woke him and Lisa up. The message sender was Mal; Leroy knew he was only hitting him up for a money opportunity. Lisa on the other hand felt Jamal was up to something, and she didn't trust his ass. She rubbed sleep from her eye, as the sun peeped through the blinds.

All she could hear was Leroy laughing and saying, "Yeah nigga, I'll see you there." She leaned her back up against the headboard, waiting for Leroy to fill her in on his plans. Leroy walked past the bed, grabbing his shoebox from the closet, and his black jeans and hoodie.

"So baby, what's up?" Lisa bit her nail, waiting for an answer. Leroy tossed the box back in its place, as he stood in front of Lisa getting dressed.

"Bae, you need to go and get LJ from Mama's and grab some shit to cook fa tonight and when I get back I'll tell you all about it." He kissed her forehead, as she held his hand tight, pulling him down, kissing him slow and hard.

"I love you, daddy, be careful."

"You betta know it mami, I love you more." He kissed her one last time before heading out of the apartment. A small part of Lisa wanted to act a fool so he wouldn't leave, but she knew that part-time job wasn't helping. She knew he had to be a man and do for his family, but her family wouldn't be complete without her man. Leroy and Jamal met at the same corner as before, loading and cocking their Glocks, waiting for the city bus.

Jamal lay his head back against the bus seat, staring out the window. Leroy taps his chest, asking about their new target.

"Muhfucka, some Asian kid from New York, started dealing X, and now erybody say he got the best Kush in the state."

Leroy nodded his head, trying to make sure he didn't miss anything about their mark. "So he gon' be by himself or what?"

Jamal looked side to side to make sure they had no eavesdroppers. "Lil bastard keep his triplet cousins wid him, bitches 'bout sumo-sized, so I set up a meeting to get some shit. One of his cousins drive and the other two his shadows."

"So how the fuck we 'posed to get the shit without getting shot?"

Jamal laughed, pointing his elbow towards the front of the bus, where about five lil niggas wid purge masks on gave head nods. "My hittas gon' take care of them while we rack up on erything in the truck." Leroy and Jamal shook hands as to agree to their plans; it seemed as if everything was cool and in place. Hopeful nothing would go wrong; Leroy still wasn't trying to kill anybody. Nevertheless, after seeing Jamal empty a clip in the white boy, he felt he would have to watch his back with his new partner.

CHAPTER 6

As the bus pulls to a stop, Jamal saw Samurai's hummer pull into the alley behind a gas station. He instructs the boys to get off around the corner and he and Leroy hop off the bus, slowly walking toward the alley. As they hit the corner, Leroy could see a medium built Asian guy, wearing red sunglasses. Beside him stood two cock-diesel looking white guys, and Lee could see the driver watching them through the rearview mirror. Jamal nods his head as he sees that his young boys are in position, and he gives them the signal to stand down for a few minutes. Jamal walks up and one of the white guys grabs him, but before he could get any closer, Leroy steps forward.

"Hold the fuck up, Rai, tell this nigga back the fuck up."

Before the buff dude could fully frisk Jamal, Samurai tells him to back off. "You lucky I know you motherfucker," Leroy can hear the slight accent, as the two shake hands. Jamal rubs his hands together, as they step toward the truck. "Whatcha got fa me today, my brother from another country?" The Asian laughs as he pops his trunk open; Leroy can see two of Jamal's boys approaching the front of the Hummer. The driver is too focused on them to notice; as one of the boys slits his throat, Leroy cocks his gun and gets ready for what comes next.

As Samurai reaches for a duffle bag in the truck, Jamal looks over his shoulder and sees one of his boys take out one of the bodyguards. The slinky boy walked up, pressed the gun to the man's neck and without hesitation, pulled the trigger. The silencer made a whistle noise, as his huge body hit the ground, and that's when the shit started. The second bodyguard goes for his gun and aims it at the boy; Leroy shoots him in the shoulder, making him fall to his knees. The Asian looked mad and confused, stepping around the truck and seeing his men dead, but before he could grab his weapon, he was down. Jamal aimed his gun at Samurai's temple and before anyone could blink, he put a cap in his skull. He motioned for the boys to leave, and as they disbursed, he and Leroy grabbed the rest of the cash and drugs from the Hummer. At this point, Leroy was speechless; he knew it was hard growing up in the Chi, but to be this ruthless was too much. Jamal wiped his fingerprints from the door handle, before walking around to the other bodyguard and shooting him in the face. Without exchanging words, he and Leroy jog down the next three blocks to a McDonald's, with the duffle bags on their shoulders.

Finally, they stopped; Jamal goes in and orders a pop with fries for him and Leroy. Still shocked from seeing all that blood, Leroy stood behind the restaurant, smoking a piece of blunt he had inside his pocket. He had a well-needed conversation with himself; this was going to be his last heist with Jamal. He had to think about Lisa and LJ; they were his future. After today, with the almost ten grand he had left, and whatever money from now, they were going to be okay for a while. Being together and okay, was better than not being with his family at all.

Jamal comes out and hands Leroy his drink and French fries, who says, "Good looking ma nigga, aye fam, we need ta talk."

Jamal shoves fries into his mouth, taking a long sip of his Cherry Coke. "Sup ma dude, ready to get yo money and go huh, can't fuck wid a nigga?"

Leroy gave a half laugh, "Naw, ain't dat, just been thinkin' my dude; this shit ain't fa me, love the money, but I love my family more, you know what I'm sayin?" Leroy sipped his Pepsi, chewing on one fry. He was praying silently to himself, hoping he wouldn't have to kill Jamal.

"Shit, real talk bruh, I feel you. I know you got lil man at home and shit, and Lisa ass ah kill me if I'on get you home safe." They both laughed.

"Shit nigga, if I die, she gon' revive me and kill me again."

They finished eating and drinking and made their way toward Jamal's little apartment. "So nigga, I got this one last lick guaranteed to make us both at least a mil apiece, no flex."

Leroy's head rose fast as he was heavily interested in what Jamal had to say. "Shit, you had me at mil, nigga, what's good?" "A'ight bet, my moms buys pills from this rich ass Cuban dude up in the hills and shit. She was high as fuck and slipped up and told me the muhfucka keep at least five mil stashed throughout the crib."

Listening at first, Leroy figured it was too good to be true, but then again, many shifty ass white people hide dirty money in the house. "So how in the fuck we 'posed to get in that bitch, bet it's gated up and shit."

Jamal lit a blunt as he handed Leroy his half the money, which was almost thirty thousand in cash and a few ounces of weed. "The nigga love young pretty girls, so I was gon' get one of my hoes to handle dat fa me, get us in and he won't eva know what hit him."

"Shit yeah, ain't like he gon' report the shit stolen." The two men shook hands, as Leroy heads for the front door, feeling like he literally just hit the lottery. Waiting for his door to close, Jamal grabs his cell phone, calling up one of his old friends. The doorbell rang as Jamal heated up a pepperoni pizza Hot Pocket, but before he could answer the person walked in. He was an older white man, with white scraggly hair and a long curly beard. "Sup Coleman." Jamal stepped to the dirty cop, handing him an envelope.

"How's shit on the street, dirtbag?" The cop opened up his package, running his index finger over a stack of hundred-dollar bills.

"As you can see, business is pickin' up, oinker; how's life taking criminals' money?"

Coleman laughed, taking a cigar from his suit jacket. "As you can see pretty fucking good, so what's the job, criminal?"

Jamal rubbed his hands together, thinking over what he was planning to do, "I need yo help settin' somebody up, maybe fifteen to life, round that area. I'on want the nigga dead, jus' put away." The cop shook his head in agreement as Jamal continued, "I'ma hit you up when we get to the spot. After I get my money, you pick his ass up and like I said, I'on want the nigga hurt or nothin' jus' locked up."

"I heard ya, I heard ya; you just don't fuck up and make sure you get the fuck out of there." Coleman stuffed the envelope into his jacket pocket, and walked out the door. Jamal was going to take care of Leroy, and then he would take care of Lisa. He picked up his phone and texted a hooker he knew personally, telling her to come over. Soon, he would have his woman back by his side. This was the only scenario he pictured her not being hurt so much about losing Leroy. He knew how much she loved Lee, but Jamal knew in his heart that he loved her more than anyone could.

Hearing a light knock, Jamal pulled off his jogging pants and opened the door. In walked a girl who resembled Lisa, from her blonde hair to her creamy brown skin. Jamal took her by her hand, pulling off her shirt. "I missed you, Lisa baby." The hooker knew exactly what he wanted, his obsession led him to dress her and call her Lisa. She kissed his neck, as he taught her and grabbed his erect dick. Jamal pressed his abs up against her stomach; ripping her skirt off, he pins her to the wall.

"You know I missed my King Mal." That was Lisa's nickname for him when they dated. He rubbed his fingers over her hard clit, pinching it as she stroked his dick, rubbing the head against her wetness. Jamal couldn't take it anymore; he had to be inside of her, moving her hand, he forces his long dick deep and the girl's body jerked. Jamal grabbed her hands, holding them over her head, slamming his dick in repeatedly as deep as she could take it. Screaming, she bit his shoulder hard. "Yes baby… I love you Mal, I fucking love you." Hearing those words put him over the top; she sounded just like Lisa used to. He pounded her pussy faster and harder, as she locked her legs around his waist. "Damn baby, shit," she moaned; she rolled her hips slow as he grinded his dick against her spot, hitting it hard one last time. He holds her tight, feeling his cum shoot inside of her. Pulling out of the hooker, Jamal threw her a thousand dollars bound in a rubber band, and told her to get her shit and leave. He couldn't see the hurt in her eyes as she slammed the door.

CHAPTER 7

Leroy picked his sleeping son up from the couch as Lisa lay there, switching through the channels. "Baby, can you grab me some water?" she yelled, taking off her pants and stretching. LJ as a two-year-old seemed to be much more work. She loved him and wouldn't change a thing.

"I gotchu bae." Leroy promised Lisa this would be the last time, and that he would tell her everything afterwards. He grabbed the water from the fridge, walked back to the couch, and he lay on her legs. "So baby, tomorrow morning I was thinking we could just pack up and leave."

Her eyes widened as she sat up, almost choking on the water. "Baby, what are you talking about, what about the apartment, work, and Mama Pearl?"

He knew she would have all these questions and he was ready to answer whatever she wanted. "Bae, we can pay it up for a few months. I'm quitting that job, I bought the mechanic shop down the street, and we can take care of Mama. No worries, mama, daddy got this."

She squealed, wrapping her arms around his neck tight. "Baby, I love you so much."

Leroy held her in his arms close, kissing her shoulder softly. "Daddy love you more, ma." He and Jamal needed the whole day to fulfill their plan, and Leroy had made sure Lisa and LJ were busy. The previous night, when he told her about the first heist only and the money, she was happier he was alive. He promised to hide the gun better and that after tonight, he would be done with Jamal.

Kissing Lisa goodbye, he also bent down, kissing LJ who was fast asleep, cuddling his Woody and Buzz toys.

"Come back to me." Lisa rubbed his cheek, smoothing his t-shirt over his gun.

"Can't get rid of me if you tried, bae." Smacking her ass, they embraced once more before he headed out of the apartment. Leroy could see Jamal standing at the end of the apartment, smoking a Black & Mild. "Sup folk?"

The two men shook hands as Jamal blew out a cloud of smoke. "Sup ma nigg, ready fa dis shit?"

Leroy tapped his hand on his Glock. "Mo ready than I'll ever be; let's get this shit goin'." The two made their way outside, where Jamal let Leroy know that the girl who would help them, would be waiting around the corner. Turning the corner, all Leroy could see was a short girl with tattoos and blonde hair. Jamal whistled and she turned, facing them. Leroy instantly stopped; she looked like Lisa. "Aye nigga, dis Caydence. Cay, dis my nigga, Lee." Leroy was speechless and just waved his hand; the girl flashed a pearly white smile. The only difference between the girl and his Lisa, was that Lisa's ass was huge and lil mama here was skinnier. Jamal could see that Leroy was taken by surprise at the resemblance between Cay and Lisa, which was part of his plan that night. Leroy's mind would be elsewhere, and he would not focus, meaning he would likely fuck up.

"Cool, so just go in there, drop this in his drink and muhfucka gon' be out a few hours. You take yo ass back to my house and wait for me to call, got me?" Cay and Leroy kept their eyes on Jamal as he talked. "Me, Lee, and Buddha gon' take care of the guards and shit then hit the vault, say nigga got two mil in there, we ain't gon' be greedy so we just gon' hit that one." Buddha was Jamal's cousin, a hothead black nigga with dreads, thought he was Mad Max from *Shottas*. He always did what Jamal told him and he needed someone like that for tonight.

"So how we gon' get there?" Leroy asked, checking his phone for messages from Lisa.

"We takin' Cay's car, we gon' wait in the back until she handle her bizness; when she give the signal, we go in." Jamal went over the plan a million times in his head; he knew what had to be done. They all took a shot of Grey Goose that Jamal had hidden in a cabinet, before heading to their next victim's estate. Leroy laid his head back on the seat as Caydence drove them to their destination; no one spoke the whole ride. He figured it was best, his nerves were already on edge and honestly, it was nothing to be said. Pulling to a stop, Leroy saw an all white house that looked like a mansion with about thirty windows. All of the lights were off, except one right next to the front door. The many trees surrounding it shielded them from the few neighbors the rich man had.

Before stepping out of the car, Caydence adjusted her breasts in her pink pushup bra, and applied more bright red lipstick. She looked Jamal in his eyes, he nodded and she got out, sashaying to the door of the mansion. Jamal grabs his cell and texts his cousin to meet them at the spot. He can see that Leroy is nervous, so he lights a blunt and passes it to him. After a few minutes, a small two-door car pulled behind Cay's Camaro. Leroy took a long drag from the Kush, watching as Jamal hopped out the car. A short chubby dude with dreads shook hands with Jamal, before revealing a silver 9mm. Jamal smiled as he and his cousin walked back to the car, Leroy glanced at the car that dropped off Buddha. He could see old ass white dude in sunglasses was driving; it was weird as fuck to him, but he brushed it off. It had been fifteen minutes since Caydence entered the man's house, and Jamal was starting to get a little worried. He was about to make the call to rush in, when Cay poked her blonde head out the front door.

Jamal looked back at Leroy, who had gripped his Glock tight with a stern, ready look on his face. "Time to do dis shit, niggas," Jamal smiled, as he headed for the front door. Caydence walked past him grinning, handing him a piece of paper. Upon entering, Jamal instructed Buddha to take the man in the basement and tie him up, while he and Lee hit the vault. Jamal and Leroy headed to the back of the house where the money vault was, the code was the man's kid's middle name.

Jamal held the paper up to the light, and typed in the name Marisol really slow and careful. When he and Leroy heard the door ding, they got excited, as the vault door opened. Buddha came from the front. His eyes opened wide, none of them had ever seen that much money in their lives. Jamal broke the silence by tossing Buddha a bag. "Nigga, stuff whatever you can in that bitch." He handed Leroy one also, as the three of them ripped the bundles of money from the shelves. Seemed to be way more than two-million dollars, but no one talked; they shoved money into the bags up to the hilt. Leroy spotted a pair of diamond earrings stashed on a corner; he grabbed them, shoving them into his pocket. Before Buddha could make his way through the house to jack more shit, Jamal pulled him aside and whispered something to him. He took the bag from Jamal, and ran toward the front door. Leroy hoisted the bag on his shoulder, but Jamal stopped him before he could leave.

"Yo nigga, let's go check and see if the muhfucka still tied up." Jamal started to walk down the basement steps.

Leroy looked confused, stepping closer to the front door, "Naw boy, fuck him; let's go, ain't got time fa dat." He turned around, and then he heard Jamal cock his gun.

"I gotta kill him, folk, he gon' come lookin' fa Cay and she gon' lead him to me soon or later, can't have no loose ends."

Before Leroy could stop him, Jamal rushed down the basement stairs. Leroy could hear the white man yelling, "No, no, please don't." He dropped the bag at the door, making his way into the damp basement. He was too late, upon seeing him Jamal put a bullet right into the man's skull.

"Fuck yo, let's fucking go."

Jamal and Leroy both ran up the stairs, but as soon as Leroy hit the top, he stopped dead in his tracks. The white man who dropped Buddha off had a gun aimed right at his face. "Freeze motherfucker, police, you're under arrest for murder and armed robbery."

Leroy didn't know what to do; he looked over at Jamal, who wore a smile on his face. "You bitch made ass nigga, you set me up."

"All's fair in love and war nigga, and I'ma be there to console her when yo bitch ass up there." Leroy rushed Jamal, tackling him into a wall, as the two men begin tussling. Detective Coleman smacked Leroy in the back of the head, with the butt of his gun.

Leroy falls to the ground and Coleman cuffs him and yells at Jamal. "Grab the cash and get the fuck outta here dumbass, and I better get paid, or your ass is next." Jamal grabbed the bag that Leroy dropped and ran out of the front door. When backup finally arrived, they threw Leroy in the back of a police car. The forensic people worked on the scene and eventually brought the man from the basement. All Leroy could do was cry; his life was ruined and he knew he had lost Lisa and LJ for good.

CHAPTER 8

Caydence hurried and gathered some clothes in a duffle bag, waiting for Jamal. She was beyond happy at the fact he'd promised they would run away together. She grabbed a few pairs of his shoes, as the door swung open. Jamal ran towards the room, rummaging through his drawers, as if she wasn't even standing there. "Bae, what you look—"

He rose up, raising his hand as for her to shut up; she backed away into the living room. Tears forming in her eyes, she sat on the edge of the couch and watched him throw papers and shit all over the floor. Jamal finally found what he was looking for; grabbing his phone charger, he plugged his phone up and quickly hit Lisa's number. He planned to lie to her before Leroy was able to call. His plans were to have her away from Chicago, before she was able to talk to Leroy. After that, he thought he'd pay Caydence, getting rid of her for good.

The phone rang five times before Lisa finally answered. "The fuck happened, is he okay?" Jamal could hear the anxiety and worry in her voice, but he still wasn't going back on his plans. He wanted her too bad and with opportunity rearing its ugly head, he refused to say no.

"Lisa, I been shot, and fuck, Lee got caught by the fuckin' twelve, baby girl, I promise I'm beyond sorry; he told me to promise ta give you da money, only if you want me too." Jamal breathed into the receiver heavily, trying to sell his story. After a long pause, all he could hear was a loud thud and baby LJ start crying loudly.

Jamal dropped the phone, grabbing as much money from the bag as he could, and threw it at Caydence. Already crying from the bullshit lies he just told Lisa, she could no longer control her anger. "The fuck you goin', nigga you promised!" she yelled, as she kicked the money across the floor. She was about to push him, when he grabbed her wrists tight.

"Looka here bitch, only thang you gettin outta me is some dick, anythang else dis ain't it feel me!" She kicked him in the balls, sprinting for the door. While cupping his sack, he ran behind her grabbing her by the hair, slamming her to the floor. "If I eva see yo hoe ass again bitch, you dead." He spat on the floor beside her, before storming out of his apartment.

Caydence cried harder, grabbing a few of the bills from the floor. She was beyond hurt by what Jamal had done to her, but sooner than later, he would know exactly how she felt. Before leaving, she left him a note, heading for the bus station; she would rather be far away than around and not have him. Jamal was walking so fast, his legs hurt. He felt bad about what he told Lisa, only because he thought she was hurt. He could see the light on in the apartment from across the street. It had been about ten minutes since they talked, and he had to get up there to see her. Forgetting about the elevator, Jamal ran up the stairs, taking two at a time.

He was about to bang on her door, when it creaked open just from his touch. Stepping in slowly, he could see her sitting on the floor, with LJ clutched in her arms.

"Lis, you wanna talk?" He moved closer to her, she stood up walking into her room; she laid her son on his father's pillow.

Kissing LJ's forehead, she closed the door, trying to be quiet as possible. As she walked closer to Jamal, he could see how puffy and red her eyes were. She hadn't stopped crying since they gotten off the phone with each other, and now she looked at him with cold eyes. "Wh- where the fuck is the money?" she stuttered, trying to keep her composure in front of him, as much as she wanted to break down. Something inside of her told her he set Lee up, but without proof, what could she do? One thing for sure, she hated him. He stepped closer to her, and Lisa grabbed Leroy's gun from underneath her shirt, aiming at Jamal's chest.

"Baby girl, calm down, I'm just here to check in you, money's at my crib." He slowly grabbed the barrel of the gun, lowering it to his side. Lisa gave in, sobbing loudly, tears flowing from her eyes. She fell into his arms as he held her tight; she hugged him back, but all she could think about was Leroy.

"I gotta call up there or sumthin', gotta go down there." Before she could grab her phone, Jamal pulled her back closer to him.

"Lis, you can't do dat, they gon' wonder how you know about it; you gon' have to just wait for him to call." She cried even harder, falling onto the couch. Jamal pulled a joint from his pocket, lighting it, he handed it to her.

Lisa hesitated, but finally took it from his hand. "I can't live without him, Mal, I know me and you have our problems, but I don't wanna be without him."

He put his arm around her shoulder. "You my nigga and so is he, I'm here fa y'all no matta what."

Lisa took a long hit off the joint, exhaling, she laid her head back on his arm. Looking towards her room door, making sure LJ was still asleep; she decided to take Jamal's advice. She hoped that Leroy would be granted a call soon, because she felt crazy being consoled by Jamal. She placed the phone on the charger and curled up on the couch next to Jamal. She figured she would wait about two hours, and then head down to the precinct. She didn't care what anyone thought; she had to see Leroy. Having Jamal there made her feel good for a while. Then she felt bad, the fact she was sitting there happy and it wasn't because of Leroy. Lisa was happy that Jamal was being so caring, and it also felt kind of weird. Jamal wasn't known for being nice, unless he was getting something from the deal. Deep down, she hoped it was because of their past that he was helping, and not just some way to get back with her.

It seemed like forever since the janky ass cop had thrown him in that holding cell. He was read his rights and then arrested. They had charged him with home invasion; he was scared and pissed off, but glad it wasn't for murder. He didn't want the cops to see him break, so he held his tears inside. His face burning with anger, all he wanted to do was put a bullet between Jamal's eyes and hug Lisa. Leroy knew she was probably going crazy by now, not having heard from him in hours. He stood up against the bars. "Aye pig, when I'ma get ma phone call?" He looked as the female officer glared at him, and then turned her head. Leroy smacked his lips as an overweight black officer carrying a donut, stepped up to the cell.

"Shut the hell up in there boy, you get it when we give it to ya." After fat ass sat down, Leroy saw Detective Coleman walk through the double doors. He had a smug look on his face as if he had accomplished something that night. He signed his name on a few papers on the fat slob's desk and strutted over to the cell Leroy was in. "Lookin' real comfy there, Mr. Burman." Leroy wanted to spit at him, but didn't want to get his ass beat in this police station or killed. Coleman paced back and forth, smiling at Leroy. "Hope you ready fa dat ride nigger, yo ass headin' up state."

Leroy's eyes widened, he didn't expect to be leaving so soon and without talking to Lisa. He knew this was a part of that weak, bitch ass Jamal's setup. A younger white female officer with huge breasts came out, handing him some paperwork. He grabbed the keys from his desk and tossed them to her. "What should I do with him, Detective Coleman?" He buttoned up his jacket, popping a Lucky cigarette into his mouth,

"Put his ass in my car, and I'll drop him off at the prison myself." Leroy wanted to resist and fight, but he knew once he got where he was going, he would call her. He went with the officer cooperatively, being shoved into the back of a squad car. Coleman stood outside of the car, smoking the rest of his cigarette; he was on the phone yelling loudly. "Just have me a fuckin' cell ready or your wife will mysteriously get pictures of what your lard ass did at your bachelor party, asshole." He ended the call, shoving his phone into his pocket; hopping into the car, he started the engine. Adjusting the rearview mirror,

Coleman looked Leroy in the eyes. "You won't be seeing that pretty lil thang for a while, boy."

CHAPTER 9

Leroy woke up as Coleman's car pulled up in front of Pontiac Correctional Facility. At that moment, Leroy let a single tear roll down his cheek. He wanted to hug his son more than anything in the world, and to hear Lisa's voice would be life right now. He noticed two armed guards standing outside the doors, obviously waiting for him. Coleman giggled as he pulled to a stop; one of the guards roughly opened the door, yanking him from the backseat. "Take his ass to the hole, feed him, clothe him, but don't let that motherfucker out of solitary for no reason whatsoever."

Leroy couldn't take anymore; he spit at Coleman's feet. "You dirty ass piece of shit, crooked ass, nothin' ass cop, hope you die bitch, you lucky I'm cuffed, hoe."

Coleman laughed harder as the two guards dragged Leroy off into the building. He threw a money stuffed envelope into the bushes for them, winked and hopped back into his car and drove off without a care. Upon entering the building, Leroy could smell the strong stench of piss and musk. He jerked away from the guards and walked on his own, observing the prison from wall to wall. He could hear men yelling threats and sexual shit at him, but he held his head high. There was no hoe in his blood at all, and he would let anyone know that if needed.

They stopped at a desk, where an elderly black female guard named Jenson handed him his jumpsuit and shoes. After changing into his prison attire, he was forced down a long hallway. He walked past three cells before they stopped; cell 5 was for him. It had a bed, shower, and a toilet. That's it, no fucking window. That alone was going to drive him fucking insane. Under law, he was required one hour of rec time, alone with the other four solitary inmates. He stood back, waiting for the guard to close the cell door. Leroy could feel his blood boil; all he wanted to do was kill Jamal. The fact that he hadn't heard Lisa's voice in almost forty-eight hours had taken a toll on him. As he lay back on his small cot, adjusting the hard mattress and pillow, he listened at the loud screams of the other inmates. A single tear fell from his eye as he pictured his son waking up and him not being there. Leroy's concentration was broken as a metal object crashed against his cell door. He jumped to his feet, seeing a buff, bald, tatted up skinhead licking his lips at him. Leroy stepped closer to the small window on his cell door, with the meanest look on his face. "Muhfucka, whateva yo hick ass lookin' fa, this ain't it, patna."

The Aryan laughed, tapping his finger on the door. "I get who and whatever I want around here nigger, you will soon learn your place." He blew a kiss at Leroy, as he walked away whistling. He wanted to do his time with no problems, but from the looks of things that wasn't going to be possible.

Jamal had taken care of most of his business before heading back to Lisa's with the money he promised. He had to hurry and get back to her apartment before she left. Lisa had called Mama Pearl to watch LJ, while she headed to the precinct to ask about Leroy. She knew that Jamal said it would be a bad idea, but she was getting restless and missed her man too much.

Mama Pearl arrived at Lisa's door fast as she could; she didn't know what was wrong, but could hear the pain in Lisa's voice. "Nah Lisa baby, you take your time, yo lil twin is safe wid me." Mama Pearl pulled Lisa in close into a tight hug, assuring her that she had their back, no matter what.

"I promise, Mama, I'll be back as soon as I can; I'll make you whatever you want for dinner tonight and pick us up some Merlot." Mama Pearl smiled hard, kissing Lisa's cheek. "His bad butt is still sleep, but his breakfast is ready in the microwave and I got you some squares in my room on the dresser."

Lisa checked her pockets to make sure she had the keys to Mama Pearl's Durango, and headed out the door. She hoped she could get what she needed and get back home before Jamal showed up. She just was too exhausted and stressed to deal with his mouth. Lisa pulled a joint from her pocket, lighting it before she drove off. Pressing her foot on the gas, she hit the joint hard, trying not to cough. Besides Leroy, this is the only thing that could calm her nerves; she had to get to her baby. She felt slightly relieved at seeing the police station, where three cops stood outside laughing and probably talking shit. Lisa drove past them turning the corner, hitting the joint a few more times. Grabbing her perfume from her purse, she sprayed herself and then the car. She made sure she didn't put on too much, but just enough. Smelling of fresh red apples, she checked her hair in the visor mirror and headed toward the station door. Lisa smiled at the cops on her way in for good measure.

Stepping towards the receptionist's desk, she grabbed her ID from her wallet. "Ma'am, hello, I'm here to see if my boyfriend was picked up last night."

Without looking up at Lisa, the homely looking, chunky Caucasian woman slapped a form on a clipboard and handed it to her. "Fill that out and it'll be a ten-minute wait for the information."

"Uhh, okay, thanks." Lisa walked slowly towards an empty chair in the corner, filling out the form. It asked for Leroy's name, date of birth, and other information to identify him. Good thing she always kept a copy of his ID; he had about three of them, always losing and then finding them. Lisa clipped his ID under the metal clamp, and signed her name at the bottom of the form. The lady behind the counter adjusted her glasses as she took the form and set it on top of a stack of papers. "You can wait in the lobby, or we have a food area. I will call your name when the information is ready."

"Thank you very much ma'am." Lisa hoped her smooth and nice demeanor would make the receptionist work faster. She was sadly mistaken. She ended up sitting in that corner playing her Kim Kardashian Hollywood game for forty-five minutes straight. Lisa finally got agitated and stepped back up towards the counter. "Excuse me miss, not to be pushy, but you told me ten minutes and it's almost been an hour. I—"

Before Lisa could finish her sentence, the woman lifted her chubby hand to the glass. "Look, I handle it as fast as I can. Sorry for the wait, but as you can see it's one of me, with two little arms and a stack of papers, how 'bout this; I put yours at the top of my list, 'cause seem like you need special attention." The woman snatched Lisa's form from the stack, and scanned it thoroughly. Grabbing her keyboard, she entered Leroy's information into the computer. Lisa could see Leroy's mug shot at the top of the screen; he was wearing what he left the house in the other night. The lady clicked the printer icon at the top of the screen, but as she reached for it, Detective Coleman grabbed the sheet from the printer.

"Well, are you a cute little thang?" He looked Lisa from head to toe. "How do you know Mr. Burman?"

Lisa didn't want to piss the cop off, but she didn't feel like playing the question game. "He's my fiancée sir, our son cried all night wondering where he was; it's not like him not to come home and I've checked everywhere else."

Coleman sat down in a chair and laughed, laying the sheet on his desk. "Sure he ain't at one of his other baby mama's houses, Miss... I didn't catch your name."

Lisa became a little annoyed at the detective's remark, but held her tongue. "My name is Lisa, sir, and I'm his only child's mother, all I wanna know is if he's here or not, please."

Coleman could see the anxiety on her eyes, as she practically begged without speaking. Coleman stood up, grabbing the sheet. Rubbing his chin as he slowly took off his grey fedora, he stepped toward the receptionist. "Hey Patty, how 'bout you take your break a little early?" The chubby lady grabbed her lunch bag without acknowledging him and disappeared into the back of the building. The detective walked from behind the counter, stepping towards Lisa slowly. "I'm only gonna say this one time and one time only, if you want your son to end up on foster care and both his parents behind bars, then be my guest and keep asking questions."

Lisa shook her head, stammering, trying to wrap her mind around what the cop just said. "I-I don't understand... what have we done wrong?"

"Go be a good mother to your son, and maybe Leroy will be out to see the little crumb snatcher graduate, as long as you keep your mouth shut." Coleman watched as she grabbed her purse from the chair, wiping the tears from her eyes. "You have a nice day nah, you hear young lady?"

Lisa walked slowly back to Mama Pearl's truck, with her mind racing. She didn't know what to do, she felt like going crazy. Something was up with that cop, but she just didn't know what. Leroy would want her to be strong and be there for LJ, but all she wanted was for her family to be back together.

CHAPTER 10

"Damn… I wish she would just listen, she so fuckin' hardhead and stubborn." Jamal paced back and forth in front of Lisa's apartment building. Mama Pearl informed him that she had left about two hours ago, and he automatically knew where she went. He grabbed a Newport from his jacket pocket and lit it, blowing smoke into the air. The large bag filled with money sat at his feet, as he stared down the road, trying to make out if he could see Pearl's truck in the traffic. Ten minutes later, Lisa pulled up with the truck filled with weed smoke. She saw Jamal as he hoisted the bag onto his shoulder; she popped the lock for him to get in. Lisa laid her head back on the seat, Jamal could tell she was high, but could also see the dried up tears under her eyes. "You good, Lis?"

She took the cigarette from his hand, without answering his question. Jamal sighed and lifted the bag onto his lap, unzipping it, revealing wads of money stuffed inside. Lisa's eyes widened as she fanned the smoke to make sure she wasn't seeing things. "All this is for me and LJ, right?" She sounded as if she couldn't believe it, so Jamal just shook his head yes. He knew she wanted to take the money and be done with him for good. After all the shit he just went through to get her, he wasn't going to give up that easily. "Yeah, make sho y'all good for a few years, lil man can go to a good school, and I'm here if you need support."

Lisa lifted her head from running her fingers through the money. "Mal, I appreciate erything you done these last two days, but right now ain't the time to try and rekindle the fucked up relationship we had." Jamal rubbed his face, trying not to blow up on her at that moment. He understood it would take longer, but all he needed was for her to forget about Leroy. Long enough for him to make her fall in love with him again.

"Look Lis, I know the timing is hella fucked up, and I promise a nigga won't push, but just know I'm not givin' up on yo stubborn ass." He leaned over and kissed her on the cheek, rubbing his hand over her shoulder. Lisa bit her lip, staring into his eyes as he got out of the truck and walked down the street. She could feel the tears falling from her eyes again; she hated herself for even thinking about getting back with him. Only she knew the sweet side that Jamal hid from everyone else. Lisa decided to hide the money in the truck. She was going to give Mama Pearl something for all of her help and for keeping the truck. Her plans were to leave Chicago for good, but without knowing anything about Leroy, she couldn't leave, no matter how bad she wanted to. Lisa rubbed a napkin from the glove box across her face, making sure her eyes weren't too puffy. Explaining the whole story to Pearl and LJ would have been harder than the lie she decided to tell them. She looked down the street for Mal before stepping inside the apartment building; knowing that she loved Leroy, but hated the thought of being alone.

Lying on his small cot, Leroy couldn't understand how anyone could get accustomed to that horrible piss smell. They fed them disgusting ass bologna sandwiches and almost curdled milk. He felt like an unloved pet; wild animals got more love and food than this.

"Aye Lee, what's yo count, homie?"

He got up standing against the bars, putting a piece of glass outside of the cell, in order to see his prison associate. "Nigga shit, I hit a thousand last night, what's yo shit?" They had made a game out of seeing who could do more pushups; four days in this hellhole seemed like four months. Leroy had to keep himself busy; when he just lay around, all he could think about were Lisa and LJ, and the fact she hadn't contacted him yet.

"Nigga, you know my fat ass only got bout three hunnid, I ain't even gon' lie," they both laughed. Counting pushups was better than the alternative of counting how many times you had to fight a nigga off your ass.

As Leroy was about to sit back on his bed, the fag ass Aryan walked past and reached his arm into Leroy's cell, grabbing his pants. "C'mere chocolate."

Leroy spun around, grabbing his arm; with a quick motion he cracked it over the cell bar, breaking the Aryan's arm. "Bitch, I told yo ass, this ain't what you wanted, but yo hoe ass tried me anyway." Leroy continued to twist the man's arm, as the guards ran over.

"Back the fuck away from the bars, inmate." The big white man screamed as if he'd gotten crushed by an anvil.

The guards yelled for the cage to be opened and rushed Leroy, throwing him to the floor of the cell. One of them cracked him in the back of the head with their nigga beater, as his body became weak. They dragged him by the arms, with his feet tripping over one another. "Drop his ass in the pit for a few hours." The warden had instructed them to take him to a special hole in the ground. It's where they put inmates deemed the most violent. With the lies Coleman told them, Leroy was prone to violence at the fullest extent. The guards stripped the shirt from Leroy's back, and tossed him into a deep, dusty, piss drenched, trench-like hole.

"Fucking pig assholes." Leroy spit in their direction as he leaned his head up against the dirt wall. Not even a week and he had already gotten on the warden's shit list.

Felt like dying with the thought of not seeing his little family again. On the verge of passing out, Leroy heard footsteps approaching his new cell in the ground. The sun beamed down into the hole, which was also a part of the punishment. Leroy could see the outline of a tall husky man; he could also see the outline of a big ass gun on the man's waist.

"Sooner you learn, the better boy, the route you goin' you won't live to get out and see your family again."

Leroy hated to admit it, but the asshole guard was right. If he had any chance of getting out and seeing Lisa and LJ, he would have to bow down to the prison rules. He had no problem with following rules, but he refused to be anyone's bitch at any point in his life. One thing was for sure, he would get what he deserved out of life, and so would Jamal.

"LJ baby, come get ready for dinner, I made yo favorite, legs and mac and cheese." Lisa felt his little body pressed up against her leg as he hugged her thigh. To be two, he was tall just like his daddy.

"Extwa cheesy, Mama?"

"Yep baby boy, just how you and Daddy like it." She kissed him on his forehead, picking him up and putting him in his high chair. He would make a bona fide mess if she put him in front of the TV, so she turned Netflix on Leroy's tablet for him.

"T'anks, Mama." LJ smiled hard, shoving a spoonful of mac and cheese into his mouth, smearing cheese sauce all over his chin. Lisa leaned up against the wall, smoking a cigarette as her son ate; she let her mind drift off thinking about Leroy. The harder she tried not to, the more images of him popped into her head. A soft knock on her door made her jerk; she wasn't expecting anyone. After the obvious threat from the cop, she decided to lay low with her baby boy. Lisa looked through the peephole and let out a heavy sigh of relief when she saw Jamal's bearded face. She unlocked the door and walked back over to her son, letting Jamal push the door open for himself.

"How you feelin', Lis?" He gently pushed the door shut, making his way over to her small sofa and sat on the arm of it, staring at Lisa. She took a long drag from the cigarette,

"Good as I'ma get, is that why you came over here?" Jamal could tell she was annoyed and didn't want to be bothered by him, but he honestly missed her. He couldn't get the thought of kissing Lisa out of his head and she on the other hand, just wanted him to do something to get Leroy back. Lisa wanted to tell him to leave, but didn't have the strength to fight with him.

"Mama me done, can I go play with Buzz 'nem?" Lisa smiled, lifting her son from his chair, and letting him run off into his room.

"Mama love you, LJ."

Poking his head out his door and baring all his teeth in a huge smile, LJ blew a kiss to his mother. "LJ love his mama."

"Lil man holding up good, I see." Jamal walked toward Lisa pulling off his jacket, revealing his muscular tatted arms. He licked his dark lips, as she stepped backward. After all the years she spent hating him for what a dog he was to her, she forgot that he was so damn fine and aggressive. "Well, I'm not gonna scare him and tell him what I don't know, best bet is to wait it out. Don't want to, but Lee woulda wanted me to be strong for our son."

Jamal shook his head in agreement with her, staring into her eyes. "I was being serious when I said I miss you, Lis."

He rubbed his fingers through her hair; Lisa closed her eyes, trying to keep her composure. She opened her mouth to tell him to stop, but when he pressed his lips up against hers, her mind went blank. Lisa didn't know if it was the loneliness or the fact he was being so sweet, but she kissed him back even harder. Biting her lip softly,

Jamal lifted her up on the wall, sliding his tongue down her neck slowly.

She was in a trance, she almost forgot about LJ being awake. "Baby boy, don't come out until Mama comes to get you, okay?" she managed to yell out in between whimpers. Jamal's hands seemed to rub over every inch of her short thick frame, as he pulled off her t-shirt. "Jamal, we can't do this." Lisa attempted to push him away, but he grabbed her wrists, sucking on her chest softly.

"We can baby, we can, let Mal take care of you. I promise, shit gon' be different."

Lisa moaned softly, wrapping her arms around his neck, sucking on his ear. "Yes daddy, and yes." Lisa pulled off Jamal's wife beater, rubbing her hands up and down his arms as he ripped off her small shorts, sliding his finger deep inside her wet vagina.

CHAPTER 11

Lisa bit down on Jamal's shoulder, grinding her hips as he fingered her faster and harder. He lifted her leg up onto his shoulder, pulling his long, hard, dark chocolate dick through his zipper. "Baby, you need a rubba?"

Lisa and Jamal kissed each other deeply, as he shoved his dick deep inside of her, making her body jerk. "I'ma pull out ma, shit... I missed this wet muhfucka."

Laying her head in his neck, Lisa rolled her hips hard and slow, moving her pussy with every stroke Jamal gave. She gripped his dick tight the way she knew that he loved it, and he gripped her waist, digging deep, the way she loved it. Lisa locked her legs around his waist as Jamal stroked deeper and harder, as she dug her nails into his neck holding him closer. "Baby shit... just like that baby... yes... yes." Lifting her up higher, Jamal puts both of her legs onto his shoulders, sliding her all the way down on his dick, making her bounce on every inch. Lisa screamed and quivered as he held her down, grinding against her spot. Jamal could feel her cream cover his dick as she got wetter, her body shook harder and she hugged him tighter. Pressing her back against the wall, Jamal slid his tongue down Lisa's chest, sucking her nipple into his mouth. "Baby ohh... I'm cummin' baby, I'm cummin'."

Jamal could feel his dick throbbing as she gripped him tighter, her pussy was so tight he couldn't contain himself from busting deep inside of her. He could feel her cum dribble down his dick as he stood there, holding her tightly in his arms. Jamal lifted Lisa's head, kissing her cheek softly, and said, "Baby you just don't know how much I love you." Her eyes opened wide, she didn't mind the sex because she was lonely, but she couldn't find herself loving him again.

"Mal, baby, let me down." She patted his shoulder softly, as he walked her over to the couch, laying her down. Jamal gently kissed her bellybutton, slowly sliding his finger over her clit.

"Baby, I know it's too soon, but you gon' see how much I love you, just watch."

Lisa rubbed his cheek as she handed him his jacket. "Thank you, Mal, really for everything, but right now baby, I can't, you should understand."

Jamal threw his jacket over his shoulder, trying not to show that he was pissed off, "Call me later, den?"

She walked over to him, kissing his cheek softly. "I gotchu boo." Jamal wanted to stay with her, but knew he had business to tend to. He made sure to text Coleman to make sure Leroy had money for commissary. He leaned forward, kissed Lisa gently on the lips and walked out the door. Lisa fell back against the wall; she couldn't believe what she had just done, but it felt so good to be so wrong. Jamal leaned against her door after it closed; he finally got her back where he wanted, and nothing would keep him from being with Lisa.

Running in her room to grab another pair of shorts, Lisa checks in on LJ. She could see him sitting at his small writing table, scribbling multiple colors in his *Toy Story* coloring book. Kissing his forehead, she rubbed his shoulder. "How about we go to IHOP and eat as many pancakes as we can, lil man?" He jumped up fast and in a hurry, grabbing for his closet door to find an outfit. Lisa loved seeing him this happy and she would make sure he kept a smile on his face, no matter how hard things got. She assisted him with putting on his shoes before walking into her room to roll a blunt.

Jamal could see his apartment was a piece of shit mess, he could also tell that Caydence fucked up some things on her way out. He hoped that would be the only thing she fucked up in his life. Kicking through the debris of old pizza boxes, pop cans, and old cigar papers; Jamal finally made it to his room. He figured he could buy any crib he wanted with the money he had, but first, he had to get shit ready for his empire. As he rubbed over his jean pockets, searching for his cell phone, Jamal got slightly agitated when he couldn't find it. The last place he had seen it was Lisa's apartment before their little fuck session. He'd been so tied up in her ass; he hadn't even thought to make sure he still had it before he left her. Jamal packed a medium sized duffle bag with a few handguns, some pictures of family, and a picture of Lisa; all that other shit was replaceable. Leaving a thousand dollars for the landlord for damages, which was way more than it was worth, Jamal left the door open, looking at the apartment one last time. Good memories, but he would make better ones in an even better place. He hid the bag behind the building; he would retrieve it after getting his phone back. This would be the last day that he would have to take a bus or walk anywhere ever again.

Jamal stopped at the store at the corner, he was cool with the Chaldean owner, and knew he wouldn't mind letting him use the phone. "Sup Singh, ma nigga."

The tall, foreign man stood up, with a beige turban wrapped tightly around his head. "Sup my friend, long time no see, my nigga." You could hear the strong accent as they exchanged stories, shaking hands; the constant ding of the door makes Jamal get straight to the point.

"Aye fam, let me use ya line right quick."

"Umm, lemme get two orders of your doubles stack chocolate chip pancakes please?" Lisa smiled at the young, bright-skinned girl taking her and LJ's order.

"Would you like coffee, orange juice, or soda ma'am?" Lisa looked over at LJ, who was too busy coloring on his menu to answer what he wanted to drink. "I'll take some coffee and some OJ for my LJ."

The waitress smiled, rubbing his shoulder. "Your order will be ready shortly, ma'am."

Lisa kissed her son's cheek; she planned to drop him off at Mama Pearl's after their breakfast. She had many things to think about and she needed a little bit of silence. In the middle of helping LJ with his second coloring sheet, Lisa felt her phone vibrate and then her animal ringtone started to play. She was enjoying the time with her son and didn't want any interruptions, but she hoped that it was Leroy somehow calling her. Grabbing for her phone, her small amount of excitement subsided as she noticed the number of one of the local corner stores. Answering with a scowl on her face, Lisa whispered with a mean slur, "Make it quick, I'm busy."

"Damn Lis always feisty mean ass, aye you seen my phone?" She smiled hearing Jamal's voice, even though she loved how he made her feel physically, she still didn't see herself loving him emotionally. The waitress walked over with their pancakes, Lisa watched LJ jump up and down with excitement as he grabbed for the syrup. "Umm nah but I'll look when I get back to the house."

Ending their conversation, Lisa poured syrup over her pancakes. LJ was halfway done with his second one, scarfing down forkfuls of chocolaty goodness. Taking her first bite, Lisa felt all of her issues fade away for a second. Chewing on those pancakes, made her think of all the good times when she and Leroy stayed up all night, got high and ate fluffy pancakes for hours. As LJ finished his last pancake, Lisa called for the waitress to bring them some to-go trays. "You ready to go see Mama Pearl, baby?" LJ grinned, wiping syrup from his chin,

"Oohh yeah Mama, today we goin' to da zoo." Lisa smiled; she loved that her baby was a happy kid, overall, that's all she wanted for him. Grabbing their food boxes, Lisa helped her son from the high chair.

"Hey Mama, I'm on my way with baby boy, I'ma bring some extra spending money for a lotta stuff from the zoo later." Lisa left a voicemail on Pearl's answering machine; she figured the old lady was in her back room, getting bonged out. As Lisa turned the corner, she had to look twice when she saw a scrawny girl, a little taller than she was, but it looked as if she could be Lisa's long lost sister. The girl and Lisa made eye contact; Lisa could see the girl's face get all screwed up. Blowing it off, Lisa continued down the busy street to drop her son off.

As she pulled into Mama Pearl's driveway, her phone rang; it was Jamazl calling again. "Sup shawty, I'm waiting fa you in front of yo building, hurry yo fine ass up."

"Boy whatever, I'll be there when I'm there." She hung up on him, helping Mama Pearl get LJ's things for their big day. "Mama loves her LJ." Lisa kissed him on his cheek, hugging him tight.

"LJ loves his mama."

"A'ight nah, girl come on, ain't like I'm takin him foreva." Lisa laughed, hugging Mama Pearl, before she handed her a purse with two thousand dollars inside. "Thank you for everything, Mama." The women hugged as Lisa hopped into the truck, and Mama and LJ got into the rental.

Before she even made it to the end of her street, Lisa could see Jamal standing outside her apartment building. Seeing his tall, chocolate, muscular body gave her the chills, but she knew what she had to do and that was stay away from him. "Bout time, damn; a nigga damn near grew a beard waiting on yo ass." Lisa climbed from the truck and stuck her finger up at him. As she strutted into the building, Jamal followed behind her, licking his lips. "Hurry up and find yo shit, I got an appointment."

Pushing her door open, Jamal smacked her on the ass. "Mean sexy ass, lemme see yo phone." She threw it at his chest as he laughed, dialing his number. Jamal could hear his ringtone echoing from underneath Lisa's couch. "Now was that so hard, sexy?" Lisa smiled as she lit a blunt, watching Jamal text a million words a minute on his phone. A faint knock on the door made Jamal's head jerk, it wasn't even his place but he was worried about who might be on the other side of the door. As Lisa went to open the door, Jamal reached for his gun and cocked it. When the door opened, Jamal's jaw dropped. Caydence stood there with a strange look on her face. "The fuck yo ass doin here, yo?" Jamal walked over to the door, pushing Caydence toward the hallway wall.

Lisa stood speechless, wondering how Jamal knew the girl who'd just mean mugged her earlier today. "Mal, the fuck is goin on?" Ignoring her, Jamal yelled at the young girl, waving his hand wildly in her face.

"Jamal, fuck you, I ain't 'bout to let you play me like this, muhfucka; if I'm hurtin', yo ass gon' be hurtin too." Jamal grabbed the girl by her throat and whispered something in her ear. Lisa didn't know what the fuck to think, but she wasn't going to stand there and let Jamal abuse this girl in front of her.

Grabbing Jamal's arm, Lisa spun him around, grabbing his collar. "Boy the fuck is happenin' right now."

Before Jamal could speak, Caydence coughed rubbing her neck. "He sat your boyfriend up, and I was there, that lying bitch did this to you."

CHAPTER 12

Her ears started to ring, and she got lightheaded. Lisa's eyes filled with tears, as she stared Jamal in his face, waiting for him to say anything. "The fuck is she talkin 'bout, Mal?" Lisa by this time had let him go, and the wall was the only thing keeping her from falling to the floor.

"Lisa baby, I'm so fuckin sor—" Before he could get the whole word out, Lisa balled up her fist tight and blasted Jamal straight in the nose. All he could do was grab his face and curl over, as she pounded him in the back repeatedly.

"You son of a bitch; how the fuck could you do this to me, I fuckin' hate you Mal! I fuckin' swear I should fuckin' kill you, you lyin' bastard." Lisa shoved Jamal into the wall, and walked back into her apartment into the bedroom. She reached into Leroy's favorite shoebox, grabbed his gun and stormed back out into the hallway. Aiming the gun at Caydence and cocking it, Lisa fought through the tears. "Bitch, if I ever see you again, you're dead, get the fuck outta my fuckin' sight." Caydence ran as fast as her scrawny legs would take her down the filthy building hallway. "And you, you piece of shit, I oughta put a bullet in yo fuckin' head, if it wasn't for my fuckin' son, I'd kill you. Stay the fuck away from me for good. I don't ever wanna see you again, Jamal, I fuckin' swear you betta fuckin' disappear."

Jamal stood up and that was the first time Lisa had ever seen tears in his eyes. "Lisa, please…" he said, with one hand clutching his face, he reached out to her with the other.

Lisa backed away into the apartment, shaking her head, still aiming the gun at his face. "Stay the fuck away from me, Mal." She slammed the door, falling to her knees; she dropped the gun. Lisa felt hurt and betrayed. Most of all, she felt like shit for fucking him, and letting him take her mind off Leroy. Grabbing her phone, she texted Mama Pearl to stay a few more days for their vacation, and to send her a picture of LJ. By the time they returned, they would no longer be residents of Chicago, Illinois.

Caydence walked down the street, crying and rubbing her neck; all she wanted was a bump. She could see a few dudes standing on the corners; she walked toward the one that she knew best. Caydence handed him a fifty-dollar bill, and he handed her the product. Before she could stow away behind a building and take her hit, she felt a tight grip on her hair. Last thing she remembered was her face crashing up against the brick wall, before Jamal poured ice-cold water on her face, waking her up. "The fuck is wrong with you bitch?"

Jamal paced back and forth, as she lay with her hands tied behind her back.

"Mal, I'm fuckin' sorry, you left me no fuckin' choice, and I'm in fuckin' love with you dammit." Caydence cried hard as Jamal laughed harder, aiming a pistol at her temple.

"Bitch, you knew what the fuck this was, and yo bitch ass deliberately fucked up shit wit me and Lisa. I oughta kill you, hoe." Jamal could see the tears flow from her eyes, but what she couldn't see was that he was crying also. Wiping the sweat and tears from his face, Jamal unzipped his pants, walking over to Caydence. He pulled his dick out, standing in front of her. She positioned herself on her knees, and kissed the tip of his dick. Jamal could feel tears drop on his shaft, as she slid her tongue up and down his dick, making it harder. Grabbing her jaw making her open her mouth wider, he pushed deeper, making her scratch his stomach for air. Moving her head back and forth, Caydence sucked on his dickhead slow and hard, rolling her tongue around it. Jamal threw his head back with pleasure, but couldn't stop thinking about Lisa. Caydence sucked and licked his dick faster and harder, Jamal bucked his hips harder, shoving his dick as far as it would go. Hearing her gag on his dick made him bust hard inside her throat. Jamal pulled his dick from her throat, pushing her head back. He left her on her knees with his cum on her chin. "Find yo way out and this time, I fuckin' mean it; stay the fuck away from me."

The first month seemed to be the hardest. Leroy had spent most of it locked away in a hole in the ground. Honestly, he preferred it. He wasn't thinking about making friends with any of these motherfuckers, no matter how long he was down for. Leroy found a rusty wire, carving Lisa and LJ into his arm. The pain had nothing on the pain he felt from not seeing them.

The guards had recently let him back into his cell, shoving his food tray under the door. "Burman, you got a visitor coming later."

Leroy's face lit up; he just knew his baby would find him. This was the first time he regretted wanting to kill himself. "Aye man, who is it, is it Lisa?"

The guard could hear the desperation in Leroy's voice, but he wasn't going to give him any satisfaction. "Sorry chump, gonna have to wait and see."

Every part of him wanted to throw the tray at the wall, but didn't want to fuck up his visit. His heart pounded, he was way too anxious to see who came to see him. "Fuck!", Leroy felt a sharp pain in his leg. The edge of the bed was sharp as shit, but nothing could fuck up his mood. After yard time, it would be time to go see his visitor. Leroy decided to shoot around for a while. Leroy ran after the ball after a white inmate tossed it across the yard. He felt like he was in a special education class, having to be separated from everyone else, along with four others.

"Aye man, lemme get that." A short, bald, dark gentleman walked slowly over to Leroy.

"It's 'bout three mo, this yo special ball or sumthin'?" Leroy waved the ball in front of the man, as if taunting him. Maybe being locked up for this short time had fucked with his mind, more than he wanted to admit.

"Boy, looka here, if I was you, I'd listen and obey." Hearing another man tell him to obey like some bitch made his blood boil.

Leroy bounced the ball a few times and turned his back, walking toward the net-less rim. "Right old man, you ain't me." Before Leroy could turn around to face him, the old man grabbed Leroy's arm, twisting it hard and pinning it behind his back.

"Old man got yo ass didn't he, nigga, you heard what I said." The man shoved Leroy to the ground, grabbing the ball and walked off towards the opposite direction.

Leroy felt like shit and his arm stung. Looking around, he noticed that no one was really paying attention to him and the old man. A part of him felt relieved that no one saw what happened, because he was embarrassed. Then again, these guards obviously weren't doing their fucking jobs, not to see the altercation. He wanted to go after the old bastard, but decided to let it go and head to the visitation room. Scanning the room, he couldn't see Lisa, or anyone else he might know. Just as he was about to leave, Leroy's thought his eyes were playing tricks on him. Every part of his body felt like it was on fire. He could feel his fists tighten and his jaw clench as his feet forced him to walk forward.

Jamal rubbed his face, holding his head down stepping slowly toward Leroy. The two guards were safely behind the glass; watching everyone hug and kiss their family members. Jamal pulled the chair out as far as it could go, looking up at Leroy standing over him. "Look nigga, if I could take it back I'd think about it, but you know how it is to love her, bruh."

All Leroy could see was red. Jamal didn't expect him to lunge at him in front of the guards. Leroy could feel his hands tighten around Jamal's throat, banging his head repeatedly against the linoleum floor. "You bitch ass nigga, I saved yo fucking life, bitch, and you take mine, and then you think you love her? Bitch, I'll kill you." Jamal struggled to get Leroy's hands from around his neck. Everything started to go dark, and finally the two guards yanked Leroy away from his victim. "Ain't shit we gotta say to each other yo, we ain't friends; we ain't shit." Leroy spat on the floor in front of Jamal as the guards shoved him towards the room exit. Of all the bold shit to do, Leroy hadn't expected Jamal to show up there. The guards made him strip naked and escorted him to the infamous hole in the ground. This was his home now and the only friend he had was himself.

"Fuck it, muthafuck it." Jamal slammed his rental car door shut. He sat rubbing his chin, examining his face in the mirror, and reaching for his piece of blunt in the ashtray. Jamal watched the sunset as he went over the fucked up events of the day. Never had he thought it would end like this. He had no idea where Lisa was going and a part of him felt he should have killed Caydence. She was a sweet girl when she wanted to be, but he didn't expect this shit from her. Having feelings for him fucked with her judgment of when to keep her mouth shut. He hoped he wouldn't have to put a bullet in her; regardless of how he treated her, that girl always came back. Jamal drove back to his house, grabbing all his guns and all the money he had stashed away.

Dialing one of his homie's numbers, he made sure they had a trap ready to do business. This was going to be his time. Even though he loved Lisa, having her around would have been a distraction from gaining his empire. Honestly, you never know how things would go, maybe she would forgive him one day. He didn't want LJ growing up without a father, but he knew that after knowing what she did, Lisa hated him. "I'll be there in about ten minutes, don't let that muhfucka leave."

The street was pitch black and the house sat alone at the end of the road. All that could be seen were the large bedroom windows, where the lights were on. The door was already unlocked, so Jamal let himself in. He could hear the faint voices of his runners, and a small boom box that lay by the door. "Boss, we in here."

Jamal walked toward a room in the back, where a man sat with a gag in his mouth and arms tied behind his back in a chair. "So Mr. Townes, I wanna thank you for your donation to my cause of being king, it is greatly appreciated. I am sorry you won't be alive to witness the greatness, but I assure you, your death will not be a waste." Jamal cocks his gun, lifts it to the man's face and pulls the trigger. That very moment, nothing else mattered except taking over Chicago.

"Thanks again, Mama," Lisa spoke into the receiver, thanking Pearl once again for keeping LJ those few days. She had packed away their entire apartment, locking all of Leroy's things into a storage unit; she refused to get rid of any of his stuff. All of the money was safely invested; she'd put it away for a better future for LJ and her. Rubbing her temple, Lisa felt stressed out and relieved all at once. That previous day she purchased tickets to Benton Harbor, Michigan, somewhere no one knew her and she knew no one. Before shutting her former apartment door, Lisa stood there and smiled a half smile. Suddenly, she felt a sharp pain in her lower stomach. She hadn't been trying to starve herself, but she wasn't eating, as she should have been.

Closing the door, she decided to stop by the ER before picking up LJ from the hotel. She knew Mama Pearl would make a big deal out of her symptoms, so it was better to take care of it beforehand.

"Yes ma'am, I've just been having harsh stomach pains."

The short fat nurse pressed down on Lisa's stomach, asking her to describe the pain better. "On a scale of one to ten."

As the nurse pressed harder in a certain spot, Lisa yelled out. "Ah damn right there a ten, shit."

The nurse left and grabbed a tray. "Okay sweetie, I'm gonna need some blood and urine." Lisa grabbed the small cup, as the nurse drew two tubes of her blood. "The bathroom is right over there, just put the sample into the slot and turn the wheel." She felt like she was waiting forever, craving for some ice chips as she lay in the hospital bed. "Ma'am, the doctor will be right with you."

Lisa sat up as the doctor entered the room, smiling holding her chart. "Ms. Chase, congratulations; you are two weeks pregnant."

CHAPTER 13

"Maaa, LJ won't share."

Lisa could hear her two boys, yelling and arguing over the joystick. She was so happy she had Tyler his own game stashed away for his birthday that weekend. Luckily, she made sure the decorator customized an authentic smoke room. Her little men were a handful and doing it by herself; she needed all the Mary Jane she could get.

"LJ, cut that damn game off and y'all get dressed for school. Who plays the game naked? Get y'all asses ready."

The realtor had found her a nice and quiet one story, three-bedroom house out in the country. She enrolled her boys, Leroy Burman Jr. and Tyler Burman, ages nine and six, in school at Countryside Academy. It was a semi-private school; they had a good system and her boys were excelling for their age. They already had smart mouths, now they questioned everything and it was hard for her not to pop them in their faces.

"Yes ma'am," they said in unison, walking toward their room.

"Mama, can I play the game first after school?" Tyler sticks his tongue out at his older brother, who pushes him into their dual bunk bed.

"I'll think about it, nah hurry up so you can eat before you leave."

LJ was smooth like his daddy and always seemed to get his way. Walking up to his mother, fully dressed, smiling and showing off his pearly whites, he asked, "Ma, can we go to Burger King, I want some sausage and cheese croissants." She laughed when she heard him say some, she knew her son could eat. The question was where the food went, because he was skinny as hell.

Lisa could hear her phone ringing inside her purse, but knew she had to help her baby boy. "Let's go, Ty baby, pick the shoes you want and let's go." Tyler was a little thicker than his brother was. Wasn't very tall, but stocky and wanted to play football. Lisa told her boys every day that they could be whatever they wanted, because it was in their blood.

"Okay now my handsome men, seat belts, check?"

"Check."

"Lunches that you packed yourselves that I hope aren't all candy, check?" Lisa looked around at both of them in the backseat after she heard no response. LJ wore a sly grin on his face. "Okay fuckers, come home hyper and doped up on cookies if you want; no game for a week." LJ smacked his lips, staring out of the window.

"Boy look at me, don't ever smack yo lips at me, got it?"

"Yes ma'am." Lisa leaned into the back seat and kissed both of her boys on their foreheads. "I love y'all bad asses, that's why I do what I do."

LJ smiled, he was always a spoiled kid, but he knew his mama didn't take shit from anyone, especially her own kids. Lisa fixed her hair in the visor before pulling out of the driveway. Her street was quiet and the neighbors were very respectable. LJ and Tyler played with a few boys that lived on the block, but their mother always taught them they were best friends as well as brothers. She pulled into the drive thru at the Burger King, checking the time. The boys had a good thirty minutes before they had to be there.

"Yes can I get three of your sausage, egg and cheese croissants and two of your hash brown nugget things, and two orange juices please?" She could see the boys in her mirror, smiling and giving one another high fives.

"Go Mama, go Mama," Tyler chanted as the voice in the box gave her the total and she drove forward.

"Now don't scarf it down, take yo time and eat, especially you, Ty." She gave her youngest son the stink eye, just as he shoved five hash brown tots into his mouth. Lisa sipped from LJ's orange juice and took a bite from her sandwich before driving off. Their school was about ten minutes away; she always made sure they were on time, not because it was school rules, but to show them a sense of time management. She wanted her boys to be great in everything they did.

Pulling in front of the school building, Lisa parked and helped her boys from the truck. Smoothing her hands over LJ's slacks and rubbing crumbs from Tyler's mouth, she kissed their cheeks one last time.

"Ma, people gon' see." LJ looked around, puffing his chest out as his mother laughed.

"Boy, you gon' always be my baby, know dat." The boys hugged their mother and shook hands, making their way into the school building. Lisa smiled; watching her little men walk together gave her the greatest feeling. She felt bad that Tyler would never know his father, but that was for the better of them both. Even with the money she had saved from the heist seven years ago, Lisa knew that she would have to work. During the day, she was a secretary for a middle class prosecutor. All day, criminals surrounded her. She always wished and hoped one day Leroy would walk through the door or she would see his name on a document. After all that time, she refused to give up on her true love. When night fell, Lisa worked at Czar's Bar. The life of a bartender wasn't the best, but she'd met many people and had many free drinks.

"Yes ma'am, Mrs. Travis, your husband will be back in the office in another fifteen minutes." Lisa spread her legs wider, grabbing the back of her boss's head. Hanging up the phone after convincing his wife he wasn't there, she rolled her hips, grinding her pussy against his tongue. He pushed her purple skirt up toward her stomach, as she held her panties to the side. "Fuck... right there." Lisa dug her nails into his neck, gripping his fingers as he repeatedly sucked her clit into his mouth. The best benefits of her job, was that she was paid well and her boss loved the taste of her sweet chocolate waterfall.

The cup of pencils hit the floor, as Lisa reached back to clutch the desk. Mr. Travis had her short thick legs, hoisted up on his broad, jet-black shoulders. She never even noticed that he came out of his blazer and shirt. Lisa tugged at his belt, as the seven-foot tall, married man stood over her, rubbing the head of his dick slowly. To be forty-something years old, he had the stamina of a man twenty-one years old. He always fucked her with such passion and force; Lisa figuratively felt her brains being fucked out. She wasn't looking for love and neither was he, but they loved the sex they had together. Lisa lifted her legs up toward her chest, playing with her pearl, slowly twisting it. Biting his lip while smiling at her, showing his perfect gap tooth smile, Tobias shoved every inch of himself inside her with one stroke. She could feel his dickhead press up against her cervix, while she grabbed the back of his neck, kissing him softly. Tobias dug his fingernails into her thighs, as they bucked together. The loud scraping of the desk legs could be heard throughout the building. Luckily, this was their day to debrief and be alone. Whenever she and Tobias were together, the only thing that got debriefed was his long, freckled dick.

"Cum for me, daddy." Lisa gripped his dick tight, sucking his lip into her mouth as he stroked faster and harder.

"Shit Lisa, shit… you know I'ma give it to you, baby." Leaning over her and grabbing her shoulders, Tobias grinds his dick deeper and harder against Lisa's spot.

"Fuck me… my Toby, yes baby… right there." Tobias speeds up, slamming his dick faster in and out of Lisa's wetness, as she screams louder. She locks her legs around his waist, rolling her hips, feeling his dick throb deep in her stomach.

"Fuucccck." Tobias yells out, as he clutches Lisa close to his chest; she feels the condom fill with his cum as her pussy muscles clench tight around his dick. "Damn you, girl."

Lisa pulls her skirt down, walking from the bathroom. "Here you go, Mr. Travis." She tossed him a towel, smiling devilishly and swaying her hips. "You need to call your wife, she sounded really worried."

Wiping his mouth and dick off, Tobias smacks his lips, "She just worried I was munching on yo ass." He adjusted his pants and belt, before putting back on his shirt and tie, staring at himself in his full-length mirror.

"Well, technically you were, and you haven't even told me the case we were working on today." She watched him fixing his clothes, biting her lip as he smiled. Tobias Antonio Travis was almost perfect, besides cheating on his wife of thirty years with a hot secretary. "It's a pending case; the department is trying to catch a kingpin by the name of King Mal. He has been moving shit in Chicago, and now they believe he has his sights set on little old Benton Harbor." He couldn't see her face, but Lisa almost forgot how to breathe. It had been almost eight years since she'd seen Jamal, and she still hated him just as much. She didn't know if he knew about their son or not, but that didn't bother her. As long as he stayed far away from her, she couldn't care less where he did his business. Didn't mean she wasn't going to help the department, she just didn't want to see him or vice versa. Lisa walked up to Tobias, rubbing her hands up and down his chiseled chest. He reached his long arms around her, squeezing her ass as she giggled. Kissing him on the neck softly, Lisa finally grabs the folder and scans over what the police have on Jamal so far. She contemplated telling her boss she knew their future defendant, but didn't want to be in the dark. Tobias walked over to her, handing her a cup of coffee, as she gave him his cellphone to call his wife.

"Don't forget to say I love you," Lisa teased him; she knew he wasn't happy, but she wasn't about to play the true role of mistress. She felt she deserved more than that. "So exactly what are they charging Mr. Tyson with?" Lisa scribbled down certain things she found important or anything Tobias said.

"Well, they had him on trafficking and distributing of an illegal narcotic, but his lawyer got him off because the witness disappeared." Lisa shook her head, she knew that Jamal had changed a lot over the years, but she didn't know he had become so ruthless. "So now they're kinda hoping he brings his ass to Michigan, so we can catch him." He handed Lisa a lit cigarette, biting her ear softly. "How about a quickie before we wrap things up?"

Lisa threw her head back and looked into his big eyes. "Nah handsome, kids gotta eat sometime." Grabbing her things, Lisa made her way toward the door.

Tobias grabbed her before she could reach the handle. Hugging her close and tight, he said, "See you tomorrow then, thickums."

Her phone hadn't rung once, but as soon as she reached her truck, she heard her Tove Lo ringtone. She figured it was her boys, letting her know dinner was late. Their bad asses usually did that. Staring at her screen, she didn't recognize the number, but was very curious. "Uhh, hello, this is Lisa." It was a faint pause, and all she could hear was someone breathing. "Well, I guess I'll hang up then, creepy ass." Before she could press the end call button, Lisa heard the voice say her name. Lisa almost dropped her phone; luckily, she hadn't started her car yet.

"Why the fuck are you calling me, you know the cops looking fa yo ass?" Jamal didn't know what to say; after all this time, she was still feisty, sexy ass Lisa. "Nigga speak, or get the dial tone, I gotta get home to my boys." Lisa hadn't meant to say boys, but she couldn't take it back; she sat for almost a whole minute, waiting for Jamal to respond.

"Lisa that's exactly why I'm here, I wanna see our boy."

CHAPTER 14

Lisa was speechless. She opened her mouth but nothing came out. How in the hell did he find out about Tyler? The bigger question was how long had he known. She laid her head back against the seat, as her head began spinning. "Jamal what the fuck are you talking about?"

Jamal laughed sarcastically, "Look Lisa, I don't have time fa ya games, all I wanna know is the truth." Things felt weird and for a moment Lisa thought someone was watching her. She started her truck and started driving toward her house. The boys caught a ride from a mom she knew and trusted. She wanted to call them, but didn't want to piss Jamal off. "Look Mal, ain't shit in Michigan for you, so yo best bet is to fuckin' leave, okay, just go."

"Yo, I'm tryin my best not to call you a bitch, ma, and now I know it's true. How the fuck could you keep my seed from me?" Lisa could hear the heavy anger in Jamal's voice, as he continued to yell at her through the receiver. "All this fuckin' time, I coulda been there for my damn son; you fuckin' hate me that much."

Lisa instantly got lightheaded. Pulling her truck over to the gas station down the street from her house, she had to catch her breath. "You piece of shit, how the fuck could you think I wouldn't hate you? You don't fuckin' deserve to know my fuckin' son, yes muhfucka, I said my son! You'll neva see him, or any fuckin' thing, so fuck off Jamal, and worry 'bout the fuckin' police afta yo ass." Lisa threw her phone onto the floor, hoping that he would hang up. She didn't want her boys to see her this way. To them, she was the strongest woman in the world, and she wanted to keep it that way. From the gas station, she could see her front porch light on. Her pit bull, Tanto ran around the gated yard, as Tyler sat on the porch bouncing his basketball.

"Hey Mama, how was work?" Tyler ran over to Lisa before she could get her whole body from the truck.

Hugging her baby boy tightly, she kissed his forehead. "It was fine, baby, now Mama gotta get outta these shoes." Tyler held his mother's hand as they walked through her glass front door. "Leroy Junior, come down so y'all can pick something for dinner tonight." She threw her body onto the couch, grabbing at her heels and yanking them off.

LJ's big, size ten feet could be heard skipping down the stairs. "Mama, I gotta finish my homework so I can play in the game tomorrow."

"Mama know baby, just rather y'all pick together than fight later."

"Yes ma'am," the boys said in unison, as they walked off into the kitchen to raid the refrigerator.

Few seconds of silence too long, Lisa walked into the kitchen to check on her two demons. "Y'all asses are way too quiet." What she saw made her heart smile. LJ was pointing to each thing in the fridge and explaining to Tyler each item.

"We almost done, Mama, LJ tryna show me what the best thing to eat is."

Lisa smiled hard, rubbing Tyler's head and kissing LJ's cheek. She could hear her phone ring from the other room. "A'ight Mama's babies, when I get back, we gon' get dinner started." They loved helping her cook and she loved them being around her. Bad asses were growing up too fast, so she cherished and valued the time they spent together. Lisa decided to go and change her clothes, while the boys decided. Their bond meant everything and she hated when they fought, but when they made up, they were like twin superheroes to her. She could read the caller ID from where she was standing, and she refused to let Jamal bully her into seeing Tyler. Grabbing her phone she turned it off, everyone important had her landline. Sliding on her tank top and night shorts, Lisa made her way downstairs just in time to hear the knock on her door.

The person knocked two more times then waited and knocked again. Lisa looked at LJ and Tyler, sitting at the table waiting for her. She looked through her peephole, and she recognized that fade from anywhere. "Babies,

Mama will be right back. LJ you run the water; Ty, you get pots that we need, okay?"

They both yelled, "Yes Mama," as she stepped outside.

"The fuck are you doin here." She kept looking back hoping the boys wouldn't come to the door.

"Why you whispering Lis, you don't wan Ty to hear us." She looked him up and down; Jamal had filled out nicely over the years.

He also noticed her ass had grown her hair longer and her eyes were more evil. "You know what Jamal fuck you, why'd you come to my house with the cops after you, I ain risking my kids fa yo monkey ass."

"Cool, jus let me in and we can talk like civilized adults." Lisa stared him in his eyes, as he smirked. She could feel one of her sons pull on the doorknob.

"Maaaa, LJ let the water overflow." Jamal's eyes lit up and he smiled harder than she had ever seen him smile before. She almost thought she saw tears in his eyes. "Lisa damn, he sound so grown."

Shaking her head as she stared at the ground, "Here I come baby, it's okay, I'll fix it." She was about to go back inside and Jamal grabbed her forearm. "Please, I promise, I just wanna meet him. He ain't gotta know shit 'til you ready, but I gotta see my mini me." Lisa could see the sincerity in his eyes, at least that's what it seemed like. "Fuckin' fine Mal, but I swear one fucked up word in front of my kids, and I'll body yo ass; I'm not playin'."

Opening the door, she told Jamal to wait a moment as she explained it all to LJ and Tyler, but mainly LJ. "Baby, he is just a friend and not even that type of friend; you hear me, mean ass?" She grabbed LJ's jaw, staring into his eyes.

"Yes ma'am."

Jamal heard Lisa knock on the door and that was his queue. As he stepped inside, he looked around at the all blue interior. Remembering Leroy was a Crip, he knew she still loved him after all this time. Luckily, he really wasn't trying to get her back; he just wanted Tyler to know him. He could see the two boys standing in front of their mother. The taller boy looked just like Leroy, from the height, to the eyes and skin color. The smaller boy, reminded him of himself at six years old; his son looked just like him. "Wasup lil men, how y'all doin'?" Jamal walked over to them and extended his hand. Both boys stared awkwardly at him, as their mother pushed them forward.

"We good," LJ said, giving Jamal some dap; Tyler shook his hand, smiling happily. Jamal immediately felt the instant connection to the small version of him.

"Tha's wasup, what's fa dinner tonight?"

LJ rolled his eyes as Tyler blurted out, "Mama knows how to make homemade rabiolis."

"Fa real that's wasup lil man, Is it okay if I get some rabiolis too?" Before Tyler could answer, LJ pulled him into the kitchen, "Yeah that's all you getting."

Usually Jamal would snap off on a kid, but he knew Lisa would kill him in her house. "Lisa you did a good job, I'm proud of you; got you two lil bodyguards." Lisa smiled and walked slowly past Jamal, "Yea thanks to you, I gotta do it alone." He could see the mean look in her eyes as she stepped in the kitchen to start dinner. While she cooked, the boys showed him their Xbox One they shared.

"Mama promised to buy me my own PlayStation for my birthday."

"Dang that's wasup, I prefer PlayStation too myself." LJ had eventually started to be a little nice, but Lisa knew he didn't want any man around that wasn't Leroy. Him being two hadn't deterred his memory of his father.

Once Lisa was finally done with dinner, she sent LJ and Tyler to wash their hands as she hit her blunt on the porch.

"Yo kids are amazing and smart as shit."

As she blew the smoke from her mouth, all she could say was, "Thanks." She wasn't trying to rekindle any type of relationship with Jamal, friendly or otherwise. "Look Mal, they got school tomorrow and it's getting late as it, so after ravioli, you gotta go."

Jamal stood in front of her staring his dark eyes into hers. "Look, I'm leaving in a week; can I at least come to his birthday party?"

Lisa thought about it, she could see her son liked him, but she didn't want LJ to be uncomfortable. Letting more smoke out of her lungs, she smacked her lips, "Fine then we can tell him the truth about you and be done with it."

Jamal smiled, "So then he can stay wid me fa while."

Lisa almost choked on the smoke from her blunt.

"Strong ain fa erybody." Jamal joked about the weed, as Lisa tried to breathe.

"Jamal, I'm sorry, don't know what you thought; ain't mean to mislead you, but the only way you can see him is if you come here."

The huge smile he wore faded quickly. "The fuck, Lisa, he mine and you see he comfortable wid me, I wouldn't hurt him." She shook her head. Putting her blunt out, she ignored him, and walked into the house with a smile. "Sooo, who ready fa raviolis?" Her sons both jumped up and down yelling.

She could see the sad look on Jamal's face as he sat at the table in between the boys. "That shole does smell good."

"You mean sure does, Jamal." Lisa laughed as Tyler corrected his father. She cringed as she thought that.

"All, right y'all eat up so y'all can be big and strong."

"Yes Mama we know, so we can be strong men." She popped LJ in the back of his head as he made his joke, imitating her voice.

"She's right you know, look at me, I ate everything." Jamal flexed his muscles as LJ and Tyler oohed and ahhed.

They stuffed their faces, as the two boys engaged in an eating contest, making a huge mess for Lisa to clean up. "Okay okay, it's a draw… jeez, when ya stomachs start hurting, don't cry to me." LJ and Tyler grabbed the plates and silverware, taking them to the kitchen. Jamal stood up, helping Lisa clear the leftovers.

"Y'all go ahead and go upstairs, but first come say goodbye to Jamal." Within seconds, the boys were running over, hugging Jamal tight as if they had known him for years.

"All right y'all behave and listen to your mama, and hopefully, I'll see you this weekend at Ty's party, if it's okay with your mother." All three of them looked at her with puppy dog eyes,

"You knew what you was doin', askin' again in front of them." She shook her head. "Fine and you better bring a gift for the both of them and me too, shit, and don't be late; it's Saturday at three."

Jamal shook his head like a happy kid. "Goodnight lil men and Lis, thank you." After shooing Jamal off, Lisa instructed the boys to bathe and brush their teeth before bed.

"Mama, he was nice," LJ said, smiling as if giving her his approval of Jamal as her boyfriend or something.

"Nah baby, he is nice, but it really isn't like that." She hugged him as he helped his little brother in his pajamas. "Where are my kisses, Mr. Burman number one and two?"

They smiled, running into their mother's arms, showering her with kisses. She would die to keep those smiles on their faces. "Goodnight Mama." LJ squeezed Lisa's neck tight as Tyler crushed her stomach. To be small, they were definitely strong. They hugged each other and hopped into their beds. Lisa smiled as the boys, covered up and closed their eyes. Without both of her boys, she knew she would probably go insane.

CHAPTER 15

"Caymalia, come here right now," Caydence yelled for her skinny-legged daughter to hand her the remote control for the television.

"Dang Mama, but it's right there next to you." Before Caymalia could duck, her mother launched a can of soda at her head. Luckily, it hit her in the shoulder as she began to cry,

"Motherfucka, don't mouth off to me I shoulda aborted yo ass." Mali had it rough; her mother blamed her for her weight gain, and the fact she was without a man. Even though she was only seven years old, she pretty much had to take care of herself. She had to cook for herself and do her own hair. During the school year, her mother threw money at her and told her to go shopping for her own school clothes. "Whatever Mama, I'm heading to Briana's house; I'll be there all night."

Caydence smacked her lips. "Lil ass prolly gay; ain't get that shit from me, though."

Caymalia ignored her mother's mean remarks and stormed out the front door. She felt sometimes she would be better off in foster care, but a part of her loved her mother. Caydence had been hurt, and she took the pain out on Caymalia. Mainly because she looked just like Jamal, and It sickened her to look at Mali. As she stepped outside, the cold Chicago air hit her hard.

"Hey girl, you ready?" Briana was her twelve-year-old friend. She was young and wild; she'd even had oral sex before. Caymalia wasn't ready for any of that, but she loved drugs. She'd started with pot, now Bri handed her an ecstasy pill.

"Heck yeah." Mali had to grow up quick and she figured since she had to act like an adult, might as well party like one. Mali popped the pill, and laid back in the huge windowless van. She could feel her body go numb and start tingling. After a while, everything went black.

Jamal didn't know that Saturday would get there so fast. He still hadn't figured out how he was going to get Lisa to let him keep Tyler. The way he saw it was that he had missed so much; it was only fair. Then again, he did get her baby daddy locked up, just to get with her. He understood why she was angry, but she could at least let him help her out with his own son and hers as well. "Aye man, how much is that PlayStation VR headset?" The cashier brought him the headset and told him it was four hundred and some tax. "A'ight lemme get that and that new Xbox Kinect you got." He could see the cashier had an awkward look on his face. "I got cash, bruh, hurry this shit up, I'ma paying customer." The boy ran off to grab what Jamal wanted, as he checked his watch. It was an hour before the party started. He had already grabbed Lisa a diamond bracelet and she let him know she had the system already for Tyler. "That will be six hundred, twenty three dollars even." Jamal paid the cashier and left the game store.

"Aye man, did you get that room ready like I told you?" He yelled at his maid, as he dodged a stray dog in the street. "I'll be back in three days; it better be ready." Lisa didn't know, but once she let him keep Tyler, he didn't plan to give him back. Maybe he would keep him for a year or two. His empire needed an heir after he was gone, and who better to be king than his own blood? He sprayed a little cologne on before making his way into Lisa's backyard. "Hey lil man, happy birthday." Jamal loved seeing the smile on Tyler's face and noticed that LJ wasn't as excited. "C'mere big bro, got sumthin' for you too."

"Whoa… Mama, he got me a Kinect," LJ screamed and hugged Jamal tightly, thanking him as Tyler opened his gift.

"Damn Mal, did you have to outdo me?" Lisa noticed the expensive gift that Jamal had bought for Tyler, but she did appreciate it.

"Mama, Mama, Mama… he got me the virtual reality headset, oohh thanks, Jamal, man this is tight." Jamal gave the boys high fives as they ran off to show their friends their new gadgets.

"So thank you again for inviting me, it really means a lot to me."

Lisa could tell Jamal was being extra nice. "What do you want Mal, don't you have to be back home soon?" She sipped from her cup, watching her boys out of the corner of her eye.

"Look Lisa what will it take for you to lemme keep Ty for a month or two?" He could see that evil look appear in her eyes again.

"I've told you, it's not gonna happen and even if so, y'all just met; he don't know you like that and you don't know him." Lisa could see that LJ was worried and watching her, so she tried to keep her voice down. "I know you don't trust me and if you want to, you can come to, I promise you won't regret it." Watching her boys play and run around her yard made her think about Jamal's offer. Maybe her son would like to stay with his father. First though, he had to find out Jamal was his father. "I'll think about it okay, just give me a few days." Jamal shook his head as Tyler ran over to them. "Hey baby, I think it's time I tell you and your brother something very important." The kids had sung happy birthday and ate cake on their way home, hyper to their parents. "LJ, come over here for a minute." Lisa could see a mean look in her eldest son's eyes, but knew she could calm him down. "So you know Jamal has been coming around a lot this week." LJ and Tyler shook their heads, looking back and forth between Lisa and Jamal.

"Well this is hard, but Tyler, Jamal is your father." Jamal smiled at Tyler, the young boy looked confused, but then ran into Jamal's arms. Lisa looked at LJ, trying to read his facial expressions. Before she could say anything, LJ ran off toward the house, slamming the door.

"LJ, open this door right now, you don't slam no door in my damn house, you lost your mind?" Lisa knew her son was headstrong like his father. LJ was upset and he usually kept his attitude for hours and even days.

"Mama that's not fair, Tyler gets to be with his dad."

Lisa almost fainted, the words her son spoke hurt her deeply. He just didn't know how much she missed his daddy. She cried every night, hugging her pillow, wishing it was Leroy. They never saw her pain, because she had to be strong for her young men. Having them kept her sane, and if anything happened to Lisa, God forbid, Mama Pearl promised to take care of them.

"LJ, I'm sorry baby, I miss your daddy too. I promise it'll get better baby, please don't shut Mama out." Lisa waited a few minutes, then she felt LJ's door open. Her son ran into her arms, as they both cried. By this time, Jamal and Tyler had come inside the house.

"Mama, is everything okay?" Tyler asked. LJ wiped his face vigorously, trying to hide the tears from his baby brother.

"Yeah lil man, everything's good, just got something in my eye." Tyler hugged his big brother tightly.

"I love you, bro, you too Mama." Lisa loved her smart sons.

"We love you too, lil head."

Jamal loved how they bonded and he hated to separate them, but he knew LJ wouldn't want to be around him as much as Tyler did. "So Mama, for the summer, can I go stay wid Jamal?" Lisa didn't trust Jamal, but she didn't want Tyler to end up feeling like LJ. "Yeah baby, but we got a lot of planning to do before then." She could see the joy on Jamal's face and the happiness in Tyler's eyes was priceless.

"This was the best birthday ever, Mama."

Jamal said his goodbyes to the boys as they put up the leftover cake. "A'ight Lis, I'll call you before I leave, and again, thank you, 'cause I know you didn't have to do this for me."

Lisa held the door open for Jamal. "It wasn't for you, it was for my son; goodnight Jamal."

Waking up with a migraine was greatly expected. Even though she had decided to let Tyler go with Jamal, she knew it would hurt LJ. She had cried herself to sleep and awakened with her eyes so puffy, she couldn't see.

"Mama, how you sleep?" Lisa looked over to see LJ lying beside her,

"I slept okay baby, did you get any rest?" She noticed Tyler sleeping on her other side, curled up with his brother's old Woody toy.

"Yeah Mama, it was nice sleeping next to you." Lisa hugged her son close as the Sunday sunshine creeped through her blinds. The plan was to sit in the house all day and she was going to show her boys how to make crepes.

"Alrighty my mighty men, head into the bathroom and brush your teeth, shower and get ready for our fun day Sunday." Before she could blink, Tyler and LJ sprinted from her bedroom. Lisa checked her messages and missed calls. Tobias had texted her to meet him that evening for a little weekend treat. She honestly preferred fucking him in the office, but was trying to inch them away from their norm. Lisa gathered all of the items to make crepes, and noticed she didn't have any butter. The boys were completely dressed, so she told them to get in the truck for a shopping trip.

"Mama, can I bring Woody?" Tyler knew he was a big boy at age seven, but he loved that damn Woody doll just as LJ did before he turned nine. The grocery store was packed and Lisa wanted to get in and get out. She never left her kids in the car alone, so she hurried them inside as she ran to the dairy aisle. Lisa knew she shouldn't have grabbed a cart, because she started putting extra shit in it she needed. "Mama, can I go over there and get some cereal?" Tyler tugged at his mother's shirt. "Please Mama?"

Lisa was looking through the sales paper, "Yes baby go ahead, LJ, go with him."

Tyler stood in front of the cereal, tapping his foot to the *Power Ranger's* song in his head. "Man Ty, pick sumthin' before Mama come and pick for us." Just as LJ started to rush his brother, he saw a few friends from school. Running to the end of the aisle to talk to them, he tried to make sure Tyler was still in his sight.

"LJ, I'm ready; I'm goin' back to find Mama." LJ looked as his brother waved a box of Fruity Pebbles in the air.

"A'ight bro I'll be right there."

Tyler walked toward the aisle where his mother was last, and stopped when he saw someone familiar.

"Sup lil man, what ya getting?"

"Hey Jamal, I'm getting cereal, you seen Mama?"

"Yea lil man, she told me come and look for you and yo brotha and she waitin up front." Tyler looked behind him; LJ was still obviously talking to his friends. He didn't know what to do, but he trusted Jamal.

"Okay, but what about my cereal?"

"I got you lil man, let's go." Jamal went to the self-checkout and paid for Tyler's cereal and the two of them disappeared from the store.

Lisa pushed her cart fast from the front of the store, scanning the aisle for her boys. She started to get nervous, until she saw LJ leaning against the Cheerios, smiling at two girls. "Leroy Junior where is your baby brother?"

She could see the worried look on his face. "Ma, he said he was going to find you; he had his cereal, he was just right there." He spun around fast, his heart pounding.

"Tyler, Tyler!" Lisa left the cart to run through the aisles; her heart dropped when she got to the front and didn't see any sign of Tyler.

"Mama, I'm so sorry, I just had seen him, Ma." LJ had tears in his eyes as Lisa described Tyler to the store security.

"Baby, it's not your fault; it's not your fault." Lisa rubbed her son's shoulders, clutching him close and tight. The store let Lisa watch the last ten minutes of security footage, she immediately recognized her baby. "Son of a bitch took my fuckin' son!" Lisa yelled and screamed as she tried to explain that the man that took her son was his father, Jamal.

CHAPTER 16

"Come on nigga, let's get it, push that shit, push it."

Leroy could feel the muscles in his arms tighten, as his fellow inmate spotted him on the weight bench. After eight years of being cooped up on solitary, Detective Coleman's bitch ass had died; the guards let Leroy roam around with the general population of the prison. "Shit yo, I'm done, need some fuckin water." Leroy had gained almost fifty pounds of pure muscle, having nothing to do but work out and play basketball. His court-appointed lawyer at his appeal meeting, told him to take a few classes. Leroy wasn't interested in bettering himself, he just wanted to either die in there fighting, or get out and die killing Jamal. Either choice was fine with him. The old raggedy television hanging on the wall in the gym was set to the news, mainly because it didn't have any other channels. Leroy was filling his water bottle at the fountain, when he heard the newscaster say his last name.

"It has been a week since the abduction of a young boy; Tyler Burman just had a birthday, is seven years of age and was last seen walking out of a Meijer with an unidentified black male." Leroy dropped everything he was holding and stood staring at the screen. "If anyone has any information, or if you see this young boy, please call in to the hotline, and to the abductor, he has a mother and big brother that misses him. Please bring him back home safe."

Leroy felt his head get dizzy and everything went pitch black. "Bro, you good, wake yo ass up; they gon' take you to the infirmary fam, get up." The last thing Leroy saw was his Lisa and LJ on the TV screen, holding each other crying. Gunn was shaking Leroy back and forth, trying to make him regain full consciousness. No one had known that Leroy had a family and he preferred it that way. Sad thing was he didn't know anything about the little boy Tyler that was missing. What he did know was that he should have been there, and he felt like he let Lisa down.

"Mr. Burman, can you tell me what today is?"

Leroy stared into the eyes of the infirmary nurse. He wanted so bad to ask them about the news, but didn't want them or the inmates in his business. "Look, I'm good, I know what the damn day and year is; I know I'm in this fucked up ass prison, now can I please go to my cell please?"

The nurse looked over to the guard who shook his head in agreement. Before anyone else could say anything to him, Leroy was storming down the hall and to Bookman's cell. Bookman was the librarian's assistant, and he knew everything about all the news that played every day.

"Aye, yo Bookie, can I holla at you fa a minute?"
The scrawny, pale-faced old man, stood up adjusting his
glasses, as he smiled. Leroy had helped him out a few
years back with a debt he owed, and now they were a
little like family. "You think you can get me some
newspapers from the last few days, it's like hella
important." Leroy paced as Bookman searched through
the old scrap papers, handing him anything that had news
about the missing boy.

"You need anything else, just holla boy, ya hear
me?" Leroy gave Bookman some dap and headed to his
cell to find out as much as he could about Tyler Burman.
The paper printed that he was last seen with a dark-
skinned unidentified male. His mind went to Jamal, and
he prayed that that punk bitch didn't take his son. He
knew Lisa would have felt something was off if Jamal
showed up to her door; his baby wouldn't just let him in
with open arms, so he hoped anyway. Leroy grabbed his
pen and paper; he decided to go up against the parole
board again. How could they turn away a grieving father
who just wants to get out and help find his son? He hoped
he could use this angle to his advantage. If his case was
approved, he would have his parole officer reach out to
Lisa. He had to let her know that he hadn't stopped
loving her and LJ. It didn't take him long to write a
nicely written two-page later. His peeps in the mailroom
would make sure it got mailed off first thing.

His anxiety to receive his letter back was killing him.
It had almost been three weeks since he wrote the parole

board. He didn't expect an overnight response, but two weeks was fucking retarded. The bell rang for count, and the cell doors cranked open. Gunn rose from his cell, which was honestly too small for the eight-foot, goliath Jamaican that ran with Leroy. Gunn showed nothing but loyalty, ever since Leroy saved him from being killed by the Aryans. Those racist bastards were trying to gang rape him and wanted to slit his throat. Leroy made a fair trade for Gunn's life; the man didn't deserve to die. Every day, Leroy told Gunn he didn't owe him anything, but every day Gunn made sure wherever Leroy was, he was there first. The short but built female guard stood before them, doing the morning count.

"Aye boss, you hear anything yet?" Gunn was just as worried about Leroy's family as he was.

"Shit, nothing yet, my nigga, shit killin me too." After the last inmate's number was yelled off, the bell rang for breakfast. Leroy could see the frail old man pushing the mail cart towards him. "Mailman, you got anything fa a boss?" Handing Leroy an envelope, the mailman just continued down the hallway, without saying anything. Ditching the breakfast line, Leroy ran back over to his cell, with Gunn right behind him. Ripping the letter open, Leroy scanned the paper as his face dropped; his homie immediately knew the results. "Fuck man… that's so fuckin' fucked up, yo this is fuckin bullshit."

Before Gunn could calm him down, Leroy was slinging things around his cell. He couldn't believe those heartless bastards wouldn't even give him a chance to plead his story. "Boss, you need to cool it, fa dem boys come and throw yo ass in the hole." Just as Leroy was flipping his bed over, the guards rushed past Gunn, making him go back to his cell as they detained Leroy. Gunn had to watch as he was dragged off back to solitary confinement, but he would make sure he helped his friend out as much as possible.

"Lisa baby, are you okay, you want me to get you some water?" Mama Pearl rubbed Lisa's forehead with a damp towel, as she lay in her bed silent. She hadn't spoken for a whole month now. LJ spent most of his time in his room, locked away from everyone else. Pearl cooked and made sure he went to school every day, while she stayed and looked after his mother. The police had no other leads on her son's kidnapping case. When she told them it was his father, they told her she had to take him to court and handle it that way. The assholes didn't understand that it wouldn't be that easy dealing with Jamal. Lisa had a complete nervous breakdown; she lost her job, but Tobias still paid for everything, seeing as he had a soft spot for her. "Well baby girl, I'm going to check on LJ." Mama Pearl kissed her cheek, and turned off her light as Lisa cuddled up with a few of Tyler's toys.

"Boy, you gon' drive yourself crazy being cooped up in here like this." Walking into LJ's room, Pearl drew his blinds; he covered his face up as if scared of the sunlight.

"Ma Pearl, I'm okay for now, just playing Ty's favorite game." He seemed real down, ever since that day. Even with the reassurance of his mother and granny, LJ felt it was his fault because he was the big brother. Lisa tried calling the number she had for Jamal; she wasn't surprised when he didn't answer. She had no idea where he lived or would take her son. Lisa just prayed that he would bring him back or call, or even send a picture. "Okay my love, make sure you play another thirty minutes, then it is bedtime okay?" Mama Pearl didn't mind taking care of the two of them, and with the state of mind Lisa was in, Child Protective Services would try and take LJ. That was something she was not going to let happen.

Caymalia laid in her bed, pissed off that her mother sold their stamps once again for liquor money. The fridge and cabinets were so bare, even the roaches seemed to be moving out.

"Heffa get in here, right fuckin' now." She could hear her mother screaming, even with her headphones on. She thought about ignoring her, but didn't want to catch another heel upside the head.

"Yes Mama?" Cay walked over to her mother's recliner chair and her mouth dropped.

"Why the fuck were you rambling through my damn room, bitch?" She had gone all through her mother's old photos and letters, looking for some evidence of who her real father was. Caydence had always told her that her father was a good for nothing drug dealer that didn't want anything to do with the two of them, especially her.

"Ma, I needed to know something. I may only be eight, but that doesn't mean I don't understand that you just spiteful and mean, because he didn't love you, but you never gave him a chance to love me." Caydence saw the pain and tears in her daughter's eyes, but she didn't care at all.

"Motherfucker, you don't fuckin' deserve anyone's love, especially his, do you fuckin' hear me, and stay the fuck outta my room, bitch." Caymalia ran out the front door and didn't stop running, until she ran into her friends on the corner. She knew that the prostitutes weren't the best of role models, but they treated her better than her own mother did.

"What's with the waterworks, lil Cay mama?" Peaches rubbed her cheek, trying to console her.

"I just can't take it no mo, Mama hate me no matter how hard I try, Peach. I give up."

The hooker looked deep into the eight-year-old's sad baby face. "How 'bout this lil mama, head upstairs and find my apartment, number four thirty eight, make yourself comfortable and I'll bring a pizza up in ten minutes." She smiled hard, a bed and food is all she needed. Besides, what's the worst that could happen from her living with a hooker?

The door was cracked open and smelled of urine and marijuana. Caymalia instantly saw the huge TV and the bed with a bunch of pillows. She grabbed for the remote and turned on the music channel, dancing around the room. The ten minutes had already passed, and even though she was hungry, she had gotten used to not eating. She was too nosy not to check out the rest of the small apartment, so she looked through the cabinets and drawers; anything to keep herself busy. One of the drawers had a small glass mirror attached to a small brown box. She pulled it out, looking behind her to make sure Peaches hadn't come back inside. It wasn't that heavy, but she could hear something moving around in the inside. Opening the box, Caymalia recognized the cocaine in the bag from when her friend, Briana, sniffed a few lines in front of her. She was very tempted to try some. Briana always told her it made her feel like she was literally floating, bragged that the feeling was much better than weed. Cay didn't want Peaches to put her out for fucking with her stash, so she just scooped a little on her finger, and quickly inhaled as she'd seen her friend do.

At first, she felt nothing, and sniffed a small amount more, shoving everything back into place. As she began to walk back toward the living room, she couldn't feel her legs. Her whole body had gone numb, as she fell to the floor of Peaches' bedroom. "Ohh fuck." It seemed like the words took forever to exit her mouth; she had never felt anything like this before, but she loved the feeling she was having at that moment. Crawling into the living room, she pulled herself onto the dusty couch and closed her eyes. Just then, she heard the door open and Peaches' purse hit the floor. "Jamal look, I know I just got some, but I need some more, King Mal, please." Her eyes opened a little, she had seen that name tattooed on her mother's thigh. Sad thing was, she was too fucking high to move or ask any questions.

CHAPTER 17

"I want my mommy, Jamal, I really miss her, you promised I can call her," Tyler cried and pouted with his arms folded. It had been a whole month since he had taken Tyler. He had bought him every toy and game system known to man, but after a while, all the little boy wanted was Lisa. Jamal didn't blame him; he didn't know how to raise a kid. In the beginning, he only took Tyler to hurt Lisa, but now he actually wanted to try to be a father.

"Ty, I told you, yo mama tired of you, so she want me to keep you for a while." He could hear his little twin smack his lips.

"But why she keep LJ and not me?" Tyler's small voice cracked, as the thought of his mother just giving him away hurt badly.

"You my boy, so you came with me, LJ might go with your granny, but for now, I got you, and I promise I won't let anything happen to you." Tyler hugged Jamal tight, as tears flowed from his face.

"Yo mama still love you, lil man, she just need a break right now." Jamal felt bad for lying to his son, but he needed him to trust him at that moment. He vowed never to lie to him about anything ever again. "So how 'bout we go and you pick yo favorite movie off Netflix and we have us a boys' night." Tyler smiled for the first time in days; Jamal would do his best to keep that smile on his face. Jamal sent one of his runners to drop a package off to one of his favorite girls, Peaches. She ran with Caydence awhile back and kept on the streets for him. Last time anyone heard of Caydence, she'd gotten fat and locked herself up in an apartment on the Southside somewhere.

His phone had been ringing during the whole movie. Jamal refused to stop and tend to his business while he was spending time with his son. Tyler was fast asleep, and Jamal knew moving him would wake him. Covering him with his Spiderman cover, Jamal called Gabby. His connect's daughter had gotten drugs from him on occasion, so he figured he could drop her a bag for a few hours. His phone light blinked repeatedly, letting him know he had missed calls and messages. Before he could check his inbox, his phone vibrated in his hand. "Yeah, fuck is so important?"

"Mal, nigga, yo shit came up short. Itchy sayin he don't know how the shit happened, but the shit was in his hands last." Jamal hung up; he had heard enough. Nobody stole from him or tried to fuck him over. No matter who it was, he would have to make an example out of them. Gabby assured him that she would watch over Tyler, and she would call him if his son woke up.

The warehouse where Jamal handled all of his business was on a deserted street, there were no neighbors. This meant no witnesses to annoy him with complaints, or more spilled blood. He drove twenty minutes in complete silence; only thing on his mind was Lisa and Tyler. The lights were off, but he could see the cars surrounding the warehouse. Without any warning, Jamal walked inside, with his gun drawn. "The fuck is the prollem, man?"

Itchy's face was swollen and bloody, his left eye was shut from the beating he had received. "Mal, I swear to God, man, the shit ain't my fault. I ain't stupid enough to steal from you, fam, on erything." Itchy spat blood and saliva from his mouth.

"So who else was wid you?" Jamal had a seventh sense when it came to people lying to him. He was under so much stress he wanted just to put a bullet in the white motherfucker's skull. However, Jamal wasn't a complete savage, and besides every man deserved to explain himself.

"Man, just my old lady, bro, but I swear she wouldn't do no shit like this, man she know better." Having met Itchy's fiend ass woman, Jamal knew if given the chance, she would rob her own grandmother.

"Where the fuck she at, nigga?" That's all Jamal wanted to know, he never wanted to kill a woman, but he would fuck a bitch up over his shit.

"Mal, please don't hurt her, man. She my baby, man."

Jamal became infuriated and shoved his gun inside Itchy's mouth. "Bitch, if you don't tell me where the fuck she at, yo bitch ass gon' eat this bullet." Itchy mumbled something, but couldn't be heard with the Glock barrel in his throat.

Pulling it out, Jamal smacked him with the gun. "Speak motherfucker."

"She down in that abandoned building on the Westside, the one we deal out of, man please don't kill her fam, she all I got."

Jamal told Beast to head over and pick up Antoinette's ratchet ass, and he would clean up the Itchy mess. "I got you, boss man." Before Beast was completely out the door, Jamal aimed his gun at Itchy's face and pulled the trigger. Blood sprayed all over his chest and face. "I'll send that hoe yo regards, stupid motherfucker." Itchy knew better. He knew Jamal didn't play about anything that belonged to him, especially his money. To have that geeking ass bitch around his shit was very disrespectful.

Antoinette was scared shitless. She and Itchy had planned on ripping Jamal off, but they had no idea that he would catch on so easily. Itchy had told her to wait it out at the house, until he came for her. He had been gon' for three hours and hadn't contacted her at all, so she had no choice but to expect the worse. "Baby daddy call me or something, I'm tryna wait for you, damn. I need a hit bad, baby." She called Itchy's phone at least every five minutes. When she heard a loud knock on the door, she knew it couldn't be Itchy because he would just walk in. She peeked out of the window and could see Beast, one of Jamal's many goons that worked for him. The door was open and had no lock, and with the other doors being boarded up, she was basically trapped. The knocking became louder and then it just stopped. She could see Beast's shadow circle around the house, and then he walked back towards the driveway. Antoinette didn't expect him to give up that easy, and she figured Itchy had to be with them for them to find her. Opening the front door, she walked out slowly, searching the yard and driveway. Before she could step back inside, she felt a tight hand around her neck. The last thing she saw was a fist flying at her face and she blacked out.

"Wake yo ass up, bitch."

Antoinette blinked her eyes, trying to adjust her sight, she saw Jamal rubbing his gun across her lips slowly. "The fuck is goin' on Mal, let me the fuck go." Tears immediately poured from her eyes, she knew exactly why she was there tied up.

"Those tears let me know, yo ass know exactly why you here."

"We sorry, Jamal, it was the dumbest shit to do, just let us go and I swear I'll get yo money."

Jamal stood up and laughed. "Bitch, I got my money hoe, just hate y'all tried to play me." Grabbing her by the hair, Jamal dragged her across the floor, throwing her on a dirty, tattered mattress that lay on the floor.

"Please don't kill me, Mal, I'll do anything."

Jamal smiled, he loved when they begged. "That's exactly what you gon' do, any and everything they ask you and as soon as you refuse, yo ass gon' be able to see yo man again." Walking off, Jamal motioned for his boys to start work on Antoinette. One of the younger ones pulled his long, skinny dick from his pants, rubbing the head slowly. Antoinette cried harder, as she grabbed the boy's dick, slowly sucking on the head. She could see the others line up behind him. As much as she wanted to fight and try to get away, she knew her chances were slim to none. Jamal would catch her and put a bullet in her head. From the looks of things, Itchy had already met his fate.

It had been long evening, but as the sun set, all Jamal could think about was Tyler. His heart was dead for everyone else, but that boy could get the world on a platter if he wanted it. He hated when shit went how it went with Itchy and his girl. That kind of shit couldn't be overlooked; he had to deal with it drastically to show others he still had that mean streak. Walking into his house, Jamal could see Gabby and Tyler lay out across the couch passed out. Waking Gabby, Jamal paid her, also dropping a little extra for her dad. As always, he knew moving Tyler would just wake him. It was already almost one in the morning and Jamal planned to stay in the next day. All his time would be devoted to setting Tyler's life up in Chicago. Even though it was hard raising a son alone, Jamal hadn't planned to send him back to Michigan with Lisa anytime soon.

CHAPTER 18

LJ rubbed his mother's cheek, as the tears flowed down his face. It was his tenth birthday and his mother was being sent off to a home. Mama Pearl was very able-bodied, but needed all of her energy for LJ. She'd tried her best to take care of Lisa, but the more days etched by, the sicker Lisa became. "I love you, Mama; just wish you would get better."

Lisa hadn't spoken a word in the past year, and LJ rebelled. His attitude got worse almost every second. The good thing was that he didn't take his anger out on Mama Pearl or Lisa, but the kids at school felt his wrath every chance he got. He was always suspended from school for fighting. Pearl even got him a psychologist. She concluded that LJ was suffering from the loss of his brother and the fact he blamed himself, forced him to become more violent. That way, he felt like he controlled every aspect of his life. The only thing that calmed him was basketball. LJ loved streetball because of the contact, but played in school, because of his cheerleader crush. Evie was everything to him. Her light brown skin and flowing jet-black hair drove him crazy when she cheered him on during the games in school. She was a part of his therapy. Focusing on her made him feel normal and he forgot all his pain and problems.

LJ kissed his mother's cheek and rubbed her gray and light brown hair from her face. "I love you Mama, I promise I'm gon' ride my bike every day to see you and I'ma take good care of Mama P, and I promise I'ma finish school and make you proud." LJ's heart warmed as a smile spread across his mom's face.

He didn't hear Pearl walk into the room, as she placed her hand on his shoulder. "She gon' be in good hands, baby, and we can see her whenever we want, it's for the best." LJ knew it was for the good of them all. Even though he was young, he had a very mature mind. Mama Pearl and LJ stood by and watched the men take his mother out in a wheelchair, placing her inside a white van. He felt so sad on the inside. Every day he heard people say it wasn't his fault, but he was supposed to be watching his baby brother. Now his family was more torn apart than before. He vowed not to let it pull him down; he wanted to do something positive with all that hate in his heart. He hoped playing ball would keep his mind off wanting to kill the bastard that took his brother and drove his mother insane. Pearl kissed LJ as he grabbed his bag and headed out the door. A few of his friends were going to meet him at the park for a small birthday get together.

To be his age, he chose to hang with the older teenagers. LJ was very tall for his age and well respected, so he had no issues hanging out at all times of the night.

As he walked down the street, listening to Meek Mill on his iPhone, LJ could see Evie walking on the other side of the road. Immediately a smile spread across his face. He didn't want her to see him staring, so he acted as if he didn't see her at all. In school she had never spoken to him, at times he felt she didn't even know his name.

"Hey, hey LJ!"

His head jerked upward, as he heard her soft sweet voice yell his name. She waved her hand, and without even checking traffic, LJ jogged across the street to her. To see her smile because of him made him feel some type of way. "Hey Evie, right? Wasup?" She blushed and rubbed her hair from her face,

"Umm, happy birthday."

His eyes lit up, for him that was the best birthday gift he could ever get. "Thank you, thank you so much." Evie handed him a birthday card and kissed his cheek. "Uhh, so you wanna walk to my lil party with me?" Without answering, she grabbed his hand as they continued down the street together, smiling.

"Yo Ty, come here man, need ta show yo ass something." Tyler had gotten a slight bit taller. Looked more like Jamal every day,

"Sup pops."

In the year and a half they spent together, Tyler grew to trust Jamal a little more than before. He even slept through the whole night without waking up crying for Lisa. "Nah, remember when I showed you them keys and the value?"

"Yeah, I remember."

Jamal laid a stack of money on the table. "Nah this right here is ten thousand dollars." Jamal could see Tyler's mouth drop. He had always spent money on Tyler, but never let him touch any of it. That was about to change. "So how long you think it would take you to spend this?"

"Shit, Daddy I'd kill the mall, flat line, and then save some; so maybe a few months." Being around thugs and Jamal twenty-four seven for a year turned Tyler from a sweet, innocent, eight-year-old into a smart mouthed, pretty boy; know it all at the age of nine.

"That's not the fuckin' answer, boy, you take this and buy more product and flip that and then you get this." Jamal walked over to a huge picture of Scarface on the wall and tapped the end of the frame. The photo moved aside, revealing Jamal's huge, walk in safe. As they walked inside, Tyler gasped at the money bound in plastic and stacked up against the wall. "Now, this is over five hundred thousand dollars, you keep yo head on straight and stay focused on yo paper and this could be all yours one day." Jamal knew it wasn't right, but he'd rather teach his son a hustle than to have him working for some white man all his life. After locking his vault, Jamal took his son to make a run with him. The more he knew the better. Jamal knew many people hated him, and he knew he wouldn't be around for long. "So I'm goin' to pick up a few keys of that girl from one of my homies." Jamal handed his son a gold nine and showed him how to cock it. "Never aim it at yoself, and never pull it unless you gon' use it, you hear me?" Without saying a word, Tyler shook his head up and down. They pulled up to a big blue house. The attached garage had two cars halfway pulled in, one behind the other. "Nah Ty, I'm finna go in here, if I call you that mean come in, if yo ass don't hear nothing, just chill until I get back."

Again, Ty just shook his head yes. A part of him felt that his life was moving too fast, but on the other hand, he loved how his dad was treating him like an adult. "I got you, Pop." Tyler sat still, cradling the gun his father handed him. His nine-year-old brain was spinning; he didn't know what to do. To him at that moment, becoming a man meant making his father proud by being the best lookout he could be. As Jamal made his way to the side door of the house, Tyler noticed a light switch on and off inside the house as if it was some kind of message. Before he could turn his head back toward his father, Jamal disappeared into the house.

Ten minutes went by slow as ever, Tyler didn't want to have to actually use the gun, but if his dad was in trouble, he would do anything. Tyler opened the passenger door, and as he walked slowly toward the side of the house, all he could think about was his mother and brother. A part of him never forgave his mother for giving him away; a part of him also didn't want to believe his mother abandoned him. Deep down, all he wanted was his family back. The one thing Jamal had constantly told him, men don't cry, men move on. The inside of the house looked dark and there was no noise. Tyler peeked in a window and saw his father's jacket lying on a table. He could see a man walking past the window with plastic in his hands and a huge machete. He immediately thought the worse. Tyler couldn't hear his father and didn't want to just bust in the door. Playing all that GTA and Saints Row actually paid off a little. Trying the doorknob, Tyler was relieved when the door slid open quietly. Aiming the gun, Tyler walked slowly around the corner. He almost dropped the gun when he saw his father bleeding on the bathroom floor.

A man in a beige trench coat stood over him with a gun yelling, "Mal, nigga, told you, yo time is up, pendejo, it's my time to reign over these streets." The man raised the gun and just as the gun cocked, Jamal opened his eyes and saw his son. Without hesitation, Tyler aimed the gun at the man's back and fired twice.

"Motherfucka, ain't doin' shit to my daddy." Running over to help his dad off the floor, Jamal informs him there's two more men in the house with them.

Jamal rubs the blood from his eyes and mouth. "Ty, get back in the car; I'll be out in a second, I promise."

Tyler wasn't trying to hear it, he refused to leave his father in the house alone and injured. "Look Pop, we in this together."

Jamal looked his son in the eye and smiled. Of all the people to have his back like this, it was his nine-year-old. "Stay behind me then; you got it, gangsta." Just as Tyler and Jamal were about to turn the corner, a gun goes off and they both duck. "Shit, Ty don't fuckin' move, you hear me?"

Tyler shook his head as Jamal crawled toward the direction of the gunshot. Lying still, Tyler tried not to shake too hard, remembering he had a gun in his hand; he hardheadedly followed his dad.

"Look at you, lookin' like yo daddy." Tyler looked up to see a built, white guy, aiming a gun at his temple.

"Fuck you, cracker." He laughed as Tyler cursed and spat in his face.

"Yo Mal, I got yo boy." The man grabbed for Tyler, yanking him so hard the gun fell from his hands.

"Nah bitch, you got this bullet." Before the man could turn around, Jamal aimed the barrel at his temple and pulled the trigger.

Jamal quickly begins wiping the blood from Tyler's cheek and head.

"Damn Pops." Running to the back, Jamal appeared with a huge duffle bag. He tossed it to Tyler and disappeared into the room again. Tyler's mouth dropped as his father cradled three more bags onto his shoulders. "Shit Pop, what about the other nigga?"

Just as Tyler began to walk toward the door, a bullet whizzed past his head. He looked back to see his father fighting with a smaller black man, with the bags still on his arms. Without thought, Tyler ran over, wrapping his arms around the man's neck, squeezing as tight as he could. The man fell to his knees; Jamal grabs a knife from his ankle and shoves the blade deep into the man's abdomen repeatedly. Covered in blood, Tyler and his father grab the duffle bags and run to the truck. The two of them rode in complete silence as Tyler replayed the events in his head. "Ty you good?" Tyler looked over at his father's confused face and he began to cry. Jamal pulled the truck over and wiped his face. "It's gon' be aight twin, promise you won't have to do anything like that again, that's what you hire muthfuckers for you feel me." He pulled his son close, hugging him. They were all each other had. They had to take care of one another, no matter what. Finally arriving home, Jamal escorted Tyler into the garage. Dumping the contents of the bags onto the concrete floor, Jamal smiled a devilish grin. "See Ty, you get half and I get half, I woulda died if you ain't come in." Jamal shoved over twenty thousand dollars in cash toward his son. He would keep the drugs for himself, over thirty keys. Jamal planned on live well for a few months, hopefully years. He would spend the excess time making sure his son was his best friend.

CHAPTER 19

"Damn Evie, baby, slow down." LJ kissed his high school sweetheart softly on the lips, as he gently pulled off her short, purple prom dress. They had been together since their first kiss on LJ's tenth birthday. It was their senior prom; Evie was full of Hennessy and couldn't keep her hands off her man.

"Baaby, just gimme what I want right now." She smiled a devilish grin, as LJ pulled off his lavender, button up shirt.

"I love you, ma."

Evie bit down hard on his lip, sucking it into her mouth. LJ picked her up as she wrapped her thick thighs around his waist tight.

"I love you more, daddy." Pulling off her thong, LJ slid his fingers down her stomach and teased her clit. Evie sucked on his neck, leaving a hickey as she rolled her hips, grinding against his fingers. LJ didn't know when his pants came off and didn't care, only thing was on his mind was Evie. Even though they were only years old, he knew that she was the love of his life.

"Give it to me, daddy." She gazed into his eyes; her light green eyes sent a spark through his body. LJ kissed her with so much passion, they both moaned into one another mouths. He put her back against the wall, rubbing his dickhead against her wet womb. Evie slid her tongue over his shoulder, kissing up toward his ear.

"Damn bae…"

She kissed his cheek, making her way to his lips as he thrust deep inside of her, making her scream, "Yes daddy yes." LJ locked his arms under hers, moving her short, thick body up and down his long wood. Evie dug her nails deep into his back, as she gripped his dick tight, taking as much of him as she could. Stroking faster and harder, he lifted Evie's leg up onto his shoulders, slamming her down on his dick harder.

"Ohh, baby damn you… baby shit, I'm 'bout to cum," Evie screamed as she gripped LJ's dick tighter, sucking his tongue into her mouth. LJ let her down, and bent her over as she spread her legs wide with her palms on the wall.

"Shit baby." LJ stroked his dick as he slapped against her pussy lips.

"Don't tease us, daddy, make me nut all over daddy dick." He loved how nasty she got when they had sex. He honestly loved everything about her, which is why he was planning a surprise after graduation.

"You know daddy got you, mami." Grabbing her waist, he slowly slid the head of his dick inside of her, tracing his fingertips up and down her spine. He could hear her moan as her body quivered, LJ held her tight as he pushed his dick deeper.

"Shit baby, shit… you know I fuckin' love when you do that." Evie raised up with her back against his chest, turning her head, kissing him softly as he held her onto his dick. LJ reached his hand in front of her, rubbing her clit softly, as she moved her pussy up and down. She could feel his dickhead throb as he pushed deeper in her stomach, making her legs shake. "Ohh papi, here I cum."

Biting his lip, LJ locked his arm around her waist, grabbed her breast with the other and slammed his dick deep and hard inside of her. Evie's body jerked hard as she moaned loud laying her head against the wall, as she slammed her pussy back on every inch of his throbbing hardness. LJ grabbed her hands, holding them tight, as their bodies moved rhythmically in unison. He could feel her body shake harder, as her walls contracted tighter. They both screamed loud, as the sound of Evie slamming back echoed throughout the room. LJ bit down hard on her shoulder, which made her cum harder as she felt the condom fill with his cum deep inside of her. She laid her head back on his chest as he kissed her forehead gently, holding her body closer to him as she quivered. "I love you so much, daddy."

"I love you even more, baby."

Their friends knew not to wait for them, as Evie and LJ lay in one another's arms in their hotel room. LJ caressed her hair, rubbing his fingers up and down her thighs as she kissed his chest softly. "Baby, I got a surprise for you." LJ kissed Evie's lips, before jumping from the bed. She rose up on her elbows watching him, biting her lip. "I was gonna wait until after graduation, but honestly, it's all I been thinking about." Evie watched him slowly walk back over to her with his arms behind his back. As he began to get on his knee, she couldn't help but scream a little as tears started flowing from her eyes. "Baby, you my heart, and everything I do I do for us; you my future, so Miss Evie Patrick, will you do me the honor of becoming my wife?"

She held her hands over her mouth. To LJ, the silence seemed to last forever. He was about to ask again, when Evie jumped on top of him. They both fell to the floor, as she kissed him. "Yes baby, fuckin' yes." He squeezed her tight, as they kissed each other, Evie cried harder. "Damn baby, this is it." She lay on LJ's chest, playing with the diamond ring on her finger. "This is the life I want, you are who I want this life with." Smiling harder, Evie climbed on top of him rubbing her hand over his dick.

"You want some more, don't you mami?" LJ rubbed her thighs, biting his lip as she squeezed his dickhead, kissing down his chest.

"Yes daddy, but first, I got something to say to mister man down there." He loved when she referred to his dick like that. She licked further down his stomach, sliding her tongue slowly over his dickhead. Sucking his dick deeper into her mouth, Evie moaned as she stared into his eyes. For them, life couldn't get any better than this.

"Boy, slow down before you knock me over." LJ ran over to Mama Pearl hugging her tight, kissing her cheek.

"I'm sorry Ma P, ya boy is just way too excited right now." Not only was it their graduation day, but LJ was waiting on responses from his top colleges. At first, his focus was basketball, but now he had to also focus on being a good husband to Evie. He had always wanted to play ball in Chicago. Mainly because that is where he was born, it meant everything to play in his hometown. It's where he learned all about the game, but Mama Pearl wanted him to stay around Michigan.

"You just can't wait to leave me, huh boy." He smirked and kissed his grandmother one last time. He and Evie planned to go to see his mother to give her the good news about their engagement.

"Mama, you know I ain't leaving for long and plus, I'll be home almost every weekend, so you can cook for me and do my laundry." She laughed as she hugged him so he could get on his way. His mother had been in a mental institution for the last eleven years. He made sure to see her whenever possible. From the smile and the way she held his hand; a part of him felt his mother still knew him. The doctors never gave a complete diagnosis for what was wrong with her, but she hadn't talked to anyone in years; just stared out of her window.

"Kiss yo mama for me, boy."

"Yes ma'am."

Evie sat in LJ's truck, hitting a joint. "Baby, so what do you think about matching shirts for graduation?"

"Yeah bae, that's a good idea." Evie could tell that LJ's head was elsewhere. She leaned over, putting the joint in his mouth, rubbing his thigh as he started the truck. "What's wrong, daddy?" He usually got silent when going to see his mother, but he always communicated with her. "Just been thinking about Ty lately, baby, wondering if I get the scholarship back home, what if he's there?"

"Well baby, he's your brother; I'm sure he misses y'all just as much as y'all miss him." He leaned over and kissed her lips, she knew how to make him feel better.

Lisa's room was small, just enough room for a bed and bathroom of her own. LJ did what he could when it came to her expenses for her private room. He didn't need any problems with anyone bothering his mother.

"Yes sir, I'm here to see Lisa Burman." The male nurse checked the visitors' list and gave LJ two passes.

Lisa sat in a corner in her rocking chair, clutching a teddy bear that LJ gave her the first time he was old enough to visit on his own. He sold all of his Legos to get her that bear. It was as if his mother knew it, because she never let it out of her sight. "Hey Mama, you remember Evie?" Lisa smiled and turned her head towards LJ and Evie as they stood by the door. Evie held their coats as LJ went and sat next to his mother. "Mama, I got some good news." He held Lisa's hand tight as she smiled harder at him; she seemed happy he was there. "First off, I might get a scholarship to play ball back home like I wanted, and also me and Evie getting married." For the first time in years, Lisa moved her lips as if she was trying to talk. This was a huge step from the usual; LJ was so ecstatic he stood up and hugged his mother close and tight. Even though she couldn't talk, her facial expressions and movements showed she understood them. Evie and LJ stayed and talked to Lisa for a few more hours before heading home.

"Baby, I'm so proud of the man you have become and I can't wait to be your wife."

LJ kissed her lips slow and hard. "I can't wait to be your husband, baby, you know I got us."

In two more weeks, they would be high school graduates and freshmen in college. With Evie's money and grades, she could go anywhere she wanted and she planned to follow her man. She loved her life and couldn't wait until after graduation to give LJ the surprise she had for him.

"Shit Pop, all I need is my lean; money, and weed, bitches follow." Tyler was on the phone with his father, walking through the halls of his former high school. He was smarter than most of the teachers there, and dropped out a month before graduation. Tyler could have been a math prodigy, but dropped out, after being double promoted the previous school year. His father didn't know why he waited until the school year was almost over, but he didn't question his son's decisions. Tyler was a man, and had proved that to his father so many years ago. He was looking for his entrée for the evening. "A'ight Pop, I'll holla at you when I leave."

At seventeen, he was his father's right hand. Tyler handled all the business and dad sat home and took care of the connects. The bad dreams about his mother stopped after the first time he killed someone. Since then Tyler's heart has been ice cold, the only person he showed emotion to was his father. "Baaeee, look at you." The skinny big booty girl ran over and kissed Tyler's cheek. He had been growing his hair for about five years. His dreads fell to his shoulders; it complimented his dark skin and light brown eyes. Besides the dimple, he was the spitting image of Jamal as a teenager.

"Where yo ass been you was 'posed to meet me out front." He grabbed her by her arm and pulled her through the building. One girl stood and watched as the girl dragged her feet trying to keep up. Tyler looked Caymalia in her face and rolled his eyes. Neither one of them knew each other; she barely talked to anyone. She had a crush on Tyler ever since she saw him four years ago. He honestly didn't know she existed, but she was hoping that one day she could change that. "Now I'ma need you to do what you did last month, go in there, grab the money and leave the suitcase, you got me." Tyler loved how this bitch did everything he asked, and all he had to do was fuck her and flaunt her around from time to time.

"Yeah bae, I know what to do." She made his drop for him and sucked his dick, before he dropped her off. On his way walking home, he saw the girl that was staring at him in the hallway. She leaned over in a car with a miniskirt on. He could see she was tricking, turning his head, he sped off down the street.

CHAPTER 20

Gunn knew his daughter was growing up, but receiving the letter that she was getting married made him want to cry. He wasn't there to see the nigga who was taking his daughter. She was his one and only child. Right after she was conceived, he was locked up; that was nineteen years ago. They kept in touch as much as possible through letters and a few phone calls a year. He didn't want anyone knowing about his daughter. Gunn had made many enemies during his lifetime, and he knew people could use her against him. Evangeline Gunn was his only weakness.

"Baby girl congratulations, when you gon' bring the boy to see me?" She knew that would be her dad's only question, but he said it a little better than she thought he would.

"Daddy, I promise I'll handle that, he met Granny and Papa already and they love him. I know you will too, Daddy." Evie gripped the phone as she talked to her father on the collect call.

"Well at least tell me the lil nigga's name, Evie."

"His name is Leroy Burman, Daddy but erybody call him LJ. I've known him since we were nine years old, he a good dude and he play ball." Evie kept on rambling as her dad's jaw dropped; he knew that had to be Leroy's boy. They talked about his kids way too often for him to forget that name. A huge smile spread across his face, he knew his homie would love this news just as much as he did.

"Baby girl, hollup for a minute, did you say Leroy Burman Jr.?"

"Yes Daddy, my LJ."

"Baby girl, that's great news, when you get ready to visit, write me and let me know. I love you, baby girl, our time is almost up." Evie didn't know why her dad's attitude changed so fast, but she really wanted to know. Sucked the voice came over the phone letting them know they only had one minute left.

"I love you, Daddy, talk to you later." Right as she said this, the phone hung up.

It felt good to know that his daughter was with someone with a promising future. He knew about LJ's record because of his stats in the papers. Leroy kept every one he could get his hands on. "Aye Lee, nigga, I got some crazy good ass news, cuz." Leroy lay on his back doing sit-ups, as he always did. If not that, it was pushups; his body was built from being in prison for over ten years. All he did was workout; he ran shit around the prison without having to lift a finger.

"What's up my nigga, how the call go with Miss Evie, yo ass getting old, nigga."

"Shit nigga yo ass right behind me old man, my baby girl getting married, and you won't even be able to guess what her last name 'bout to be." Leroy stood up after seeing the look on Gunn's face go from excited to serious.

"Shit nigga, you know I ain't no good at guessin' games, spit that shit out."

"My baby said her LJ plan on taking good care of her. Nigga, yo son 'bout to be my son-in-law." Leroy's body felt hot and then went numb, and he fell against the bedframe.

"Nigga, are you fuckin' serious, don't play wit' me, fam."

Gunn shook his head up and down. "She gon' bring him up here in a few weeks, nigga, ain't you glad yo boy doin' good as fuck? Bro, that's a good thing."

Leroy didn't know how to feel, he was happy that his son had found love, and happy his son was marrying his best friend's daughter. What bothered him was that his son and obviously, his baby Lisa had no idea where he was, or that he was locked up at all. Even if they did, they'd made no effort to try to communicate with him.

He hoped when his son came, he would be able to talk to him. He would love to find out what happened to Lisa and the matters with Tyler. Some word around prison was that Jamal took him and raised him, either way; Jamal would pay for everything he put his family through.

"Shit nigga, hell yeah that's a good thing, I'm glad we gon' be even more family then we already is, my nigga." Leroy and Gunn shook hands as the bell rang for them to hit the yard.

"Mama, you woke? I bought your favorite." Caymalia walked into her house, the usual rank smell of fish and urine hit her. She figured her mom was just ignoring her as she always did. No matter how bad her mother treated her, Caymalia always made sure her mother had food and cigarettes; even the occasional Popeye's two can dine special her mother loved so much. "Ma, I know you hear me, damn, I gotta be back to work in an hour." As she made her way to her mother's room, Caymalia could smell shit. "Uggh Mama, I know you ain't shit on yoself again and think I'm 'bout to clean it up." Pushing open her mom's door, Caymalia dropped the food and ran over to her mother. She could see her skin was purple, and she was ice cold. Remembering something from health class, she checked her mom's wrist and neck for a pulse. "No Mama no, don't you dare fuckin' leave me alone, Ma, damn you." She grabbed the phone as tears fell down her face, dialing 911. "Yes, I have an emergency, my mother isn't breathing please send someone, please!"

As they wheeled her mother's body out the house, the officer talked to Caymalia, handing her a tissue. "So ma'am, do you have any other family or friends to stay with tonight?" She shook her head yes, before grabbing her overnight bag and heading to Peaches' house.

"Girl, I need a hit so bad right now."

"Yo ass know you ain't getting none of mine." Peaches sat on the couch with a Colt 45 in her hand.

"Well, can you call yo dude for me?"

She looked at Caymalia's face as she gave Peaches the puppy dog eyes. "Bitch here, he ain't finna yell at me, you call him yo damn self." Caymalia grabbed the phone, pressing the talk button on the phone. "Sup Peach, what you need?" Caymalia knew that voice and she became speechless. Peaches snatched the phone, told Tyler to bring over three of them and hung up.

"Bitch, the fuck is wrong with you?" She pushed Caymalia out of the way, as she stormed into the kitchen.

"Shit girl, my bad, I heard his voice and my ass forgot how to talk."

"Damn I forgot, Mal's son been running for him lately, he is yo age ain't he? Aww, look at you hoe ass got a crush."

"Fuck you bitch, takes one to know one."

"Damn right, and I know a few." They laughed as they waited for Tyler to come. Caymalia would rather Peaches get it from him for her, but her ass was being a bitch and wanted to see Cay squirm. She was sad about her mother dying, but not as sad as a normal eighteen-year-old girl would have been. Her mind was more focused on how she was going to look in front of Tyler. There was a slight knock on the door; she slowly walked over to open it as she smoothed out her skirt. As she opened the door, her hazel eyes met his dark brown gaze.

"Hey Ty." She reached her hand down to give him the money, but he pushed his way inside.

"Where Peach at?" He recognized her from school; he just knew she wasn't the one the shit was for.

"Umm, she sleep, but I got the money, uhh… it's for me."

He pushed the shit back down into his pocket. "The fuck you mean it's for you, yo ass go to school wit' me shorty, you don't need this shit." Tyler was a drug dealer, but he refused to sell to anyone from his school, or even his age period, refusing to help a teenager fuck up their life.

"Uhh… first of all, no disrespect Ty, but you don't know me, or what I deal with, you don't know what I need." He laughed and started to walk toward the door. She tried her best to stop him. "Wait, where are you going?"

"I'm leaving, have a nice night, ma." Caymalia started to cry, she just didn't want to fight anymore. Tyler turned around and watched her lie back on the couch as her face her turned red and she cried harder.

"Shit, what's wrong man?" Before he knew it, he was sitting down with her talking about their mother issues. After about an hour, they found out they had more in common than they expected. "Well look, how 'bout this, next time you feel like you need a hit, call me so we can talk." This was the first time Tyler was thinking of someone, besides himself.

The next few weeks seemed to pass by fast. Caymalia used money she saved to bury her mother, giving her a nice small funeral. Tyler was nice enough to come, he and Cay were spending a lot of time together. Mostly in his small apartment, he helped her get off the drugs. She hit a blunt every now and then, but she had been clean from cocaine for a month. It felt good to have a reason to smile that didn't involve putting something up her nose.

"Babe, you hungry?"

Tyler didn't expect to have any feelings for Caymalia at all, but ever since that night, he just wanted to be around her all the time. He didn't know if it was love, or the way she held his dick in her throat, but she was different from all the other girls he dealt with. "Naw baby girl, come back to bed for a few minutes."

She walked back over to the bed, swaying her hips. "So Ty, are you gonna sign up for school with me this week?" Caymalia had been trying to get Tyler to sign up for a few classes at the community college. He had made her stop tricking; to a certain extent, Tyler saved Caymalia's life. Otherwise, she would have been working on the streets or somewhere overdosed on drugs.

He hugged her close and tight kissing her lips softly. "I gotta make a run baby; I'll think about it some more I promise." He had been telling her that for days, but honestly he wasn't trying to go back to school. All he wanted to do was hustle. It's what he was good at. "I'll see you later on tonight baby girl."

Caymalia had completely forgotten about the fact that Jamal might be her father; she was too wrapped up in the good feeling that came from being with Ty.

"Pop, I'm heading that way now; I'll have yo money and a bonus when I get home." One of Jamal's runners had stopped answering his phone and never dropped off Mal's money.

Tyler loved handling problems such as these. He didn't want to be labeled as "Trigger Ty", but that's whom people saw him as. He never hesitated to shoot anyone, and Tyler didn't shoot to wound, he shot to kill. People knew not to fuck with him and his father and that's how he liked it.

He could see Carter standing on the corner, shaking hands with a bunch of other niggas. Tyler parked around the corner, and walked over to where Carter stood. "So nigga, you don't hear yo phone?"

When the other niggas saw Ty, they all disbursed from the area and left Carter alone. "Shit my bad, Ty, running my mouth. I ain't even been paying attention to my phone."

"So where Pop's shit at?" Tyler got straight to the point.

"Man, it's at the crib; I was on my way there after I left here; niggas owed me money, you know how that is."

"Yeah nigga, 'cause you owe me, now go get my shit." Carter walked slowly to his car, as Tyler hopped into the passenger side. They rode to Carter's house and Tyler waited for him to run in the garage. It seemed like he was in there for about twenty minutes, so Tyler decided to go inside. Cocking his gun, he walked slowly inside the garage. "Nigga, the fuck is taking you so long."

Tyler could see Carter crouched down on the floor, as he rose up; he aimed his gun at Tyler's face. "Nigga, I hate to have to do this, but yo daddy ain't shit and you ain't either. Y'all muhfuckers ain't right, and I'm done taking orders from you bitches."

Tyler laughed at him, and Carter looked confused. "Fuck is so funny, lil nigga."

"If you gon' shoot somebody, shoot 'em nigga, the whole speech was weak and you right though; you done taking orders from me and my daddy." Before Carter could move, Tyler pulled the trigger and put a bullet right between his eyes. "If you gon' kill somebody, just do it, stupid muthafucka." Grabbing the duffle bag from Carter's trunk, Tyler texted his dad he was on his way. The bus could take him back to his truck. Caymalia would be waiting, but she would be okay for the night. Maybe he could take a class to get his diploma and go to college for accounting; he didn't have to stop hustling, he could do both.

CHAPTER 21

The last two months had been a blur. LJ had received a full ride to play basketball to the school in Chicago, just as he wanted. He and Evie had gotten a small apartment off campus, kind of like the one his parents stayed in when he was a small child. Evie wanted to get her business degree, so she could get her own hair salon. Even though LJ promised her that she didn't have to work, she always wanted to own her own salon, and he wanted her to have everything she wanted and more.

"Baby, I don't feel so good."

The move to Chicago had taken a toll on the both of them, adjusting to a new home and new people. Evie had been sick for a couple days, but their insurance hadn't kicked in yet.

"Vee baby, let me just take you to the hospital, you know you need it." LJ hated seeing her in any kind of pain; he wanted to know what was wrong with her. "Fuck dis, mami, I'm taking you, let's go." Scooping her into his arms, he walked her out to the car, and drove her to the emergency room. It took them an hour to be seen, and thirty minutes for the doctors to know what was wrong.

"Well congratulations, Mr. and Mrs. Burman, the baby is just very picky and hungry. You just need to eat more and drink more water, and you will be fine." The nurse left the room as LJ turned to Evie and smiled. "Baby, damn... a baby." He kissed her cheek as she hugged him tight.

"I'm so scared baby; we just got into college, are we even ready for a baby right now?" LJ could see the worry in her eyes,

"Baby, I promise I got us, you ain't got nothing to worry about, I love y'all." He rubbed her stomach as she smiled hard, kissing his forehead.

"I love you more, daddy." LJ drove Evie home after buying a huge double cheeseburger meal from Burger King. She devoured it within minutes, as he grinned, watching her eat.

"I'm finna head to the school for some practice, baby, if you need anything or feel any kind of way, call me."

"I promise I will, daddy, have fun." Kissing his fiancée, LJ headed out the door.

He hadn't had a complete tour of Chicago; he honestly he didn't care to do so. It was his hometown, but he had no good memories of his childhood. He and Evie met in Michigan, he went to school there, his mother was there, and he couldn't forget Mama Pearl. Chicago offered the one thing that no one else could, the feeling of kicking ass on a Chicago basketball court. It's what he craved more than having Evie as his wife. Driving to the college gym, he rode past the corner store. Outside stood over ten niggas in black hoods, for a second, he thought he saw Tyler, just an older meaner version. He felt his foot push down on the brake pad. Hopping out of the car, he walked over to the crowd, rubbing his eyes.

"Ty-Tyler is that you?"

The dreadhead boy pushed his hood back from his face, with a scowl on his face. "The fuck is askin'..." Before he could finish his sentence, he stared harder at the face of the man in front of him. Tyler turned to his goons, who all had reached for their guns. "Y'all back down; it ain't nun but my bitch ass, grown ass brother. Muthafucka LJ, nigga, is it really you?"

"Tyler, shit... nigga, the fuck happen to you after all these years? Nigga do you know mama went crazy after you disappeared."

Tyler's face was confused as he pulled his brother into a tight hug. "Nigga, shut the fuck up and hug yo lil brother, a nigga missed y'all." They hopped back into LJ's truck as they sparked up a joint. "Bro, what you mean Mama went crazy? Pop told me she gave me away 'cause she needed help raisin' me and shit."

"Bro, I swear, we looked everywhere fa you, my nigga for real. I felt like it was my fuckin' fault all this time and look at yo ass, the fuck you doing here." Hitting the joint hard, Tyler looked over at his brother.

"Nigga, I run shit, I'm the prince of Chiraq. Pop keep a steady flow and I keep shit cool on the street." They laughed. "So what yo ass doin' back in Chicago?"

"Nigga, I got a muhfuckin' scholarship to play ball, like I always wanted and now I just found out I'm 'bout to be a daddy, boy."

Tyler clapped his hands together hard. "Nigga, that's three reasons to turn the fuck up." Tyler didn't know how to react at seeing his big brother for the first time in over ten years. However, he knew being mad wasn't going to solve anything. He would rather they catch up and he could show his brother around his city.

"Lee, nigga, I'ma show you how we do it big nigga style." Tyler took his brother to every bar that was open. The two brothers each took five shots of Hennessy for every year they were apart.

LJ had to admit it felt good as hell to be around his baby brother. Things were so crazy after their mom got sick; they just gave up. "Bro, fa real, all this time I figured Mal had you, Mama just lost it one day, I don't 'een know what happen."

"Shit nigga, it is fucked up he never let me call ah nothing, but I knew Mama and you missed me. I done became a thug ass drug dealer, Mama would be pissed." The boys laughed, downing their last two shots.

"Ty, shit… tomorrow you can meet Evie and shit, maybe after I find a way to forgive Mal, I'll come by and speak."

Tyler followed his brother toward the door. "Shit fa real, Lee, I was mad too at first, but then I came to an understanding. He was helping me be a man, and even though I missed so much of yo life and Mama's, shit seemed to work out for the better." Tyler looked intently at his brother's face.

LJ didn't agree with that at all. "Ty, honestly I can see how you feel that way, but nigga, Mama ain't been right since that shit happened, and I know you still feel something for yo mama, bruh."

It took Tyler a minute to respond and LJ could tell his response wasn't sincere at all. "Yeah, I do but then again, she just gave up, Lee."

"But she sick, 'cause she couldn't live without you, Ty, how you think that made me feel?" LJ leaned closer to his brother, nudging his arm. "Nigga regardless, you still my lil brother, ain't shit change that. Now one mo drink, and then I gotta get home to wifey." They both were very drunk and couldn't drive, so they decided to walk as far as they could get.

As they walked down the street, holding one another up by the shoulders, they staggered back and forth trying to stay upright. "I fuckin' love you, my nigga." Ty laid his head on LJ's shoulder as they walked up towards Tyler's apartment door. The lights were on and even though it was two in the morning, people were still awake. LJ had completely forgotten about basketball practice, this day had more surprises than he could handle. It meant everything to have his brother back. They weren't kids anymore though; they had lives and couldn't change now. LJ would try to fix the bond between he and his brother, but deep down he knew he would always hate Jamal. He would pray that Jamal wouldn't come between him and Tyler. "Shit lil bruh, yo ass is heavy, should I knock or nah?"

Tyler grabbed his phone from his pocket and texted Caymalia. He knew her ass would be up waiting for him, no matter what time it was. Few seconds later, the door swung open and the bright-skinned, tall girl stepped on the porch in some boy shorts and a tank top. Kind of shocked him, she resembled his mother a little. "Thanks whoever you are, I know Ty can knock 'em back." She grabbed his arm, helping him inside.

"No problem, lil mama, I'm his big brother; my name LJ, you can call me Lee." Caymalia's eyes lit up, after all the conversations about his family they had in the short time they were together, she never thought she would actually meet his brother. "Oh shit, I'm Cay, nice to meet you Lee; I know y'all had a ball."

Looking over at Tyler sprawled on the couch, LJ laughed. "Yeah he took most of 'em, I'ma see y'all tomorrow at the game though, good night, later bruh."

Tyler smiled and waved his hand. "Get some rest, baby, got a big day tomorrow."

"LJ you had me worried sick, don't ever stay out this fuckin' late again; you know how I get." Before LJ could get all the way into the house, Evie was yelling and swinging at him. Grabbing her by the wrists, he pulled her close, kissing her slow and hard.

"Bae, calm down; I got some crazy good ass news, sit yo fine pregnant ass down and let me get ya ear for a minute." Evie pushed him one last time, trying her best not to smile as he led her to their bed.

"Betta be something good, make me kill yo ass before the baby get here, chump."

He kissed her softly on the forehead. "On my way to practice, I saw this dreadhead thug nigga standing on the corner." Evie's face looked all confused and screwed up, she began to speak, but he put his finger against her lips. "Baby, it was my lil brother, Tyler, baby. I been wit' him all night, I missed practice, but he wanna meet you tomorrow at the game."

She jumped on top of him, kissing him hard and slow. "Oh my goodness, baby, I'm so happy for you. I know you're excited, I'm sorry I hit you in the head, daddy." She rubbed his cheek as he grinned. "I just thought you was out there wit' some cheerleader bitch."

LJ gripped her thigh, sucking on her shoulder. "Baby, you my one and only cheerleader."

"You bet not say that otha' word." He smirked as she kissed him harder. "I love you, daddy, don't dare scare me again."

"I love you more, mami, I ain't goin' nowhere, I promise." Evie fell asleep naked on LJ's chest; he kissed her forehead as his drunkenness wore off. All he could think about was his brother. He knew Lisa would be happy as fuck to see him, but he would have to be smart about it. The first thing he had to do was take care of Jamal. Somehow, he would make him pay without hurting Tyler.

"Baby, you got yo lucky socks?" Evie stood at the bathroom door as LJ lined up his goatee. Helping him get ready for his game was doing everything while he sat in the mirror.

"Yeah baby, I already got erything; just need you to look pretty and make ya man a sammich." He smiled and popped her on her ass as she giggled. After finishing off his ham and cheese melt, LJ and Evie left for the basketball stadium.

"Baby, you ready to kick some ass?" Evie poked LJ in the side as he parked the truck.

"Hell yeah, baby, making my statement tonight; erybody gon' know my name."

He loved the game, just as much as he loved Evie and their unborn child. LJ could hear the loud people in the stadium as he put on his number thirty four jersey. Tyler and Caymalia sat with Evie, they had front row seats. The game started and LJ was in his own world. Dunking over guys taller than him and making every lay-up he attempted. Every time he made a pass, his teammate made the basket. With LJ as captain, they blew out the competition. Looking into the crowd, he could see the smiles of his fiancée and brother. Hearing the audience chant his name was the best high in the world. Checking the board after the buzzer, LJ's team had won, 89 – 34.

"Good game, Burman." The coach congratulated him as Evie ran into his arms.

LJ looked for Tyler, but he had disappeared. Caymalia was sitting down with her face buried into her smartphone. "Baby, go sit wit' Cay; I'll be right back." She kissed him as he headed towards the front of the building. LJ could see the back of Tyler's head, as he stood there talking to a taller black man with a hood over his face. Walking over to his brother, LJ tried not to be disrespectful. Tyler looked over saw his brother waiting for him and waved him over, "Lee, bruh, you killed shit my nigga real talk; yo ass always had them skills. Hey, you remember Mal?"

CHAPTER 22

Before LJ could answer, Caymalia was running towards them yelling, "Lee, Evie throwing up something crazy, she askin' for you."

Jamal had stepped closer to Caymalia, he thought for a moment his eyes were playing tricks on him. "Umm, what's your name, light skin?" Tyler laughed as his father stared at Cay.

"Uh, I'm Caymalia, but people call me Cay." Trying to hide his expression, Jamal turned to his son. "Youngin', I'll see you at the spot later on tonight."

"A'ight Pop, later." Tyler pulled Caymalia close as they headed for his truck.

"Wonder why yo daddy was looking at me all funny, baby."

"Shit, Pops just got good taste, like his boy." He grabbed her ass, making her squeal. "So you wanna make this run wit' me, or you wanna go home?" Tyler rubbed Caymalia's thigh, as she rolled a joint.

"I can go wit' you, bae, den we can hit up Sonic's and get me a shake." She grinned and made a funny face as he pulled over to a white house with three motorcycles parked out front. "I'll be right back." Biting her cheek, Tyler jumped out of the truck. All he had to do was pick up a package and drop it off to his dad. Simple as hell, then he could get high and fuck his girlfriend.

"Zoe, you got the shit ready?"

"Yeah, baby Mal, it's on the table, tell yo daddy he betta have all my paper too, ah I'ma pop his ass."

Tyler laughed, and threw the fat Puerto Rican a wad of money. "Nigga, not if I pop you first." He walked back out to the truck, where Caymalia sat with the joint lit in her mouth.

"Did it go straight, baby?"

Staring at her, she just seemed to glow. "Yeah mami, it's straight; let's get you that shake, so you can gimme yo shake."

"Baby, I don't know what was wrong; I think it was that nasty stadium food." LJ held Evie's hand as she walked into their apartment. He tried to pay attention, but his mind was still on Jamal. If it hadn't been for Evie getting sick, he would have cussed him the fuck out.

"Bae, you prolly need to lay down and get some rest. I seen you jumping up and down all excited today, you was reppin' for ya man, I love you for that."

"You betta love me, bae, I'm 'bout to get fat soon, you betta love all of me."

He pulled her closer to him, kissing her chest and neck softly. "I'ma always love all of you, baby."

LJ decided that next morning he would call Mama Pearl and let her know Tyler was alive and well. Loving seeing his brother, he hated the fact that he was a drug dealer; LJ knew nothing good could come out of that. After watching Evie doze off to sleep, LJ decided to walk to the corner store and grab some snacks. There were a few thugs standing out front, but LJ paid them no mind. He wasn't a punk, but he knew that as long as he kept to himself, he wouldn't have any problems. Apparently, there were a few fans from the opposing school in the store; they started to say slick shit to LJ.

"Nigga preppy ass been in Michigan, playin' wit' dem white boys, nah he wanna play in the hood."

"Muhfucker made me lose a lotta fuckin' money in that game tho."

LJ paid for his chips and Lil Debbie cakes, and continued to walk towards the exit door. Not to his surprise, the young thugs followed him from the store. One of them threw a can at his feet, at an attempt to scare him. "Look lil niggas, this ain't what y'all want, ya feel me." As he turned around, the boys didn't notice Tyler standing behind them. LJ smiled and sat his bag down on the floor. Luckily, they were out of sight of the store cameras. "Yo punk ass need to learn a lesson."

Before the young nigga could swing, Tyler let off a shot in the air. All the boys' heads swung around. "You muhfuckers got three seconds to get the fuck away from my brotha; y'all know wassup."

Each one of them stared at Tyler. From the scared look in their eyes, LJ could tell that the boys knew exactly who his little brother was. "Shit Killa, we ain't 'een know; our bad, G." The boys backed away slowly.

LJ smirked. "Damn, lil Ty got clout in these streets."

Tyler walked over to his brother and they shook hands. "Dese lil niggas always tryna fuck wid people bruh; it's Gucci tho, but you don't need to be out without no burner after dark. You lucky my ass was out here." Tyler lifted a small paper bag in the air. "Cay lil feisty ass get mean if she don't got no papers." Reaching underneath his shirt, Tyler handed his brother a small .38 handgun. "I feel betta knowing you got it on you, bruh."

LJ felt proud, though worried, he put his arm around his brother's shoulder as they walked back to his apartment. "So on the real, exactly how is Mama doin'?" LJ was wondering if Tyler would ever ask.

"Right now she stayin' in a hospital, in the psych ward, but I been payin for her to have a private room. Mama ain't crazy like dem other muhfuckers in there."

As they reached LJ's stoop, the boys sat down to talk more.

"You think she remember me?" Looking in his brother's eyes, LJ could see the sincerity. It warmed his heart to know that his brother hadn't turned his humanity completely off.

"How could she forget, Ty? Nigga, you meant a lot to both of us, if I was tender I'da broke down cryin' when I saw you." They both laughed as the door creaked open behind them.

Evie was standing there in a robe smiling, as she saw LJ having a moment with his brother. "Baby, you want me to make y'all anything?" She waved her hand at Tyler, as he gave her a head nod.

"Naw bae, I'm 'bout to be in there in a second."

Tyler stood up as he and LJ gave each other shoulder hugs. "A'ight bruh, lemme get home fa Cay think I'm out fuckin' or sumthin', her crazy ass."

"Good to have somebody to go home to tho, don't it?"

Before walking off, Tyler turned around, tapped his waist with his finger, and waved goodbye to his brother. LJ did the same, letting his brother know he was grateful for the protection, but he knew if Evie found it, she would shoot him with it.

Caymalia had been having bad dreams for about a week. After her mother's death, she wasn't sleeping that much, but being with and around Tyler made everything better. All of a sudden, her mind started to play tricks on her. At first, she just brushed it off, figured she was having bad side effects after quitting cocaine cold turkey. However, the dreams she had seemed so real, she didn't even want to close her eyes. Seeing Tyler lying in a puddle of blood hurt her, even though it was a dream, or more like a nightmare.

"Baby girl, sorry it took me a minute, seen LJ at the sto', nigga almost got his ass beat."

She giggled, hopping off the couch, jumping into his arms. "It's cool, daddy, long as yo ass came home, I ain't gon' throw no tantrums." Tyler kissed her slow, sucking on her tongue. Caymalia loved him, but didn't know how to say it. She had feelings for him way before they were together. Even though she stayed with him and they acted as boyfriend and girlfriend, she knew the kind of man he was. The whole time she had known and obsessed over him, Tyler never committed to anything; she didn't want to change him. She just loved the time they spent together.

"How 'bout some of dat shake, mami?" She bit his lip, helping him out of his jacket and clothes, before grabbing his hand and leading him to their bedroom. Tyler knew Caymalia was feeling him much more than just fuck buddies. A part of him loved being in control, making her wait and work for it, how he did shit. Nevertheless, deep down he knew that she was the only girl that got him. They could sit and talk about any and everything without judgment. Just in the two months they were kicking it, she knew secrets even Jamal didn't know. Tyler wanted to be a hard ass thug, with steel around his heart, but he was falling for her.

"Si papi." Her Puerto Rican, five foot seven ass drove him crazy when she batted her almond-shaped green eyes and licked her full lips, talking Spanish.

"I love it when you talk that shit, baby." He picked her up, laying her on the bed. Before he could get his pants off, Caymalia pulled his dick through his boxers. "Damn ma, you ready ain't you?" All she did was smile before swallowing his dick into her mouth.

"You betta know it, papi."

Tyler grabbed a handful of her hair, sliding his dick in and out of her mouth. Cay reached her hand down between her legs and began playing with her clit. "Shit baby…" he moaned as she was lifting her head, rubbing his dick on her lips, Tyler looked deep into her eyes. She grabbed his dick with both hands, sucking on the head hard and slow, deep throating his dick repeatedly as he threw his head back, trying to keep his composure. "Fuck baby, bend yo ass over."

Grinning, she turned around, crawling toward the headboard as her ass jiggled. Tyler crawled up behind her, rubbing his dickhead slowly, before rubbing against her clit softly. Caymalia grabbed the headboard, bouncing her ass up and down, "Like this daddy?"

"Just like dat, baby girl." He slid his fingers up and down her back slowly, gripping her waist tight, pulling her back onto his hard dick.

"Mmm just like dat, daddy." Caymalia spread her legs wider, arching her back as Tyler grabbed her neck. As he pushed deeper inside of her, she rolled her hips, slamming her pussy back as hard as she could. "Ooh Ty... papi, te amo mi amor." Tyler knew one or two of those words meant love, and hearing her say that made him fuck her harder.

"Damn Cay... baby throw dat pussy, baby... fuck me back." Ty may have been skinny, but he was very strong. He lifted Caymalia off the bed and turned her around, facing him. Sliding her back down on to his dick, Tyler lifted her legs up onto his shoulders, sucking her tiddy into his mouth.

"I love you, Ty, I can't hold it in anymore, daddy." She could feel his dick deep in her stomach, as she dug her nails deep into his back.

"Shit Cay, ain't neva loved nobody, but you got me baby, I love you too."

Wrapping her arms around his neck tight, Cay kissed his lips softly as he held her down on every inch of him.

"Fuck papi… right there, don't stop." She could feel her chest pressed hard against Tyler's; he locked his arms under her thighs, digging deeper inside of her. He could feel her body trembling in his arms, as she got closer to reaching an orgasm. "Ohh shit… damn you, Killa." He went crazy when she called him by his street name; she loved that beast inside of him.

"Take it baby, fuckin' take it." Lifting his head, she kissed him hard, sucking on his tongue as if sucking his dick. Tyler slammed her down harder, as his dick throbbed inside of her; she shook harder as they came together. Caymalia could feel Tyler's hot cum shoot inside of her. He held her down, grinding inside of her, as her pussy walls clenched his dick. "Shit mami, I feel dat shit."

"I bet you do, daddy, shit… 'cause I fuckin' feel you."

Tyler was so wrapped up into Cay; he hadn't heard his phone ring. Picking it up, he had five missed calls, he knew it could only be Mal. He didn't want to stop her from kissing his neck; the after sex high was the shit. If it wasn't for his business partner and father blowing his phone up he would have turned it off, and fucked Cay again. "Mami, I gotta go see wassup wid Pop." She poked her bottom lip out and pouted.

"Okay baby, I'll be here, finna smoke and try to walk to the kitchen." She smiled as he kissed her lips, biting her cheek softly.

"Later, baby girl."

She lay back and her head started spinning. Being there was the best feeling in the world. Tyler knew his father was probably worried about the business transaction. Normally he was supposed to report back with his every move, but ever since Caymalia was in the picture, these last two months he hadn't been as focused as he should have been.

For safety reasons, his father's crib was just ten minutes away, good walking distance in case of emergencies. That pussy was still on his mind, so he was trying to keep his dick under control as he stepped into his father's house. Jamal was counting money, separating the stacks with huge rubber bands. "Sup lil nigga, where yo ass been?" He could tell his father wasn't in a good mood, but he was feeling too good to care.

"Shit Pop, I been with Cay, erything straight ova here?"

Mal stood up, walking over to his son. "Nigga, even if it wasn't, yo ass nowhere to be found; it's 'bout time you let that lil bitch go." Before he knew what he was doing, Tyler could feel his finger on the trigger of his gun.

CHAPTER 23

"What nigga, speak?" Jamal was in his face and even though he wanted to, he kept his hand under his jacket.

"Look Pop, I know I been lacking, but shit's cool, just been wrapped up in Lee bein' around and me and Cay getting along good as fuck, and as good as money feel, it can't suck my dick."

Jamal backed down, rubbing his chin, grinning at his son, the spitting image of him as a young nigga, minus the long ass dreads. "My bad fa trippin youngin', shit just been hectic and you all I got, so just be more available, ya hear me?" They shook hands, and then Mal threw his son a stack of hundreds and a few keys. "Just the usual, until you let me know you need more."

"Cool Pop, aye; you ain't wanna fuck Cay or nun, did you?" Tyler laughed, he was joking but his father's expression didn't show any sign of laughter. "Shit, if you did, yo, that shit ain't happenin', sorry Dad." Jamal leaned onto his desk, fingering his beard. "Ty, what's her mom's name, or did she not mention her parents?"

Tyler sat in the recliner beside his father's desk. "Uhh shit, her mom died few weeks after graduation, and she ain't never know her dad, why you ask?"

"Damn, her mom died fa real, that's fucked up; her name wasn't Caydence, was it?" The look on Tyler's face let Jamal know he was right. He didn't want it to be true, but she could have been his daughter. Thinking about it, her name had his name in it, which was some crazy shit that Caydence would do.

"Dad, the fuck are you tryna say to me right now?" Tyler was getting agitated; he didn't like anyone playing games with him.

"Well, dependin' on the timeline, shit, she might be yo sista. Her mama was hella obsessed wit' me around the time y'all was born and we was fuckin' heavy."

Tyler stood up and shook his head. "Hell nah, Pop, fuck dat shit; she can't be, I'm out." He refused to believe the first girl he ever had feelings for, was his half-sister.

"Baby, you wanna say anything to Daddy when I call him? He really is excited about knowing the sex of the baby." Evie wobbled through the house with the phone in her hand. Her father was scheduled to call her in about thirty minutes. They never had long to talk, so she had to get everything she had to say out quickly. LJ and Evie were more than excited to find out they were having a little boy. Naming him was the problem; LJ didn't want to name him Leroy or Tyler, so maybe her father could help.

"Nah baby, just give him my best, and let him know we gon' be there for Father's Day if possible."

"Okay daddy, remember no onions in my omelet."

"Yes ma'am, sexy chunky ass." She hated when he made fat jokes about her baby belly. This was her sixth month of pregnancy; she was trying her best to do things, but LJ would stop her. School was going great; he was the best captain the school had seen in years. Evie knew she was in good hands. Many people expected her to be damaged goods because her father was never around, but she turned out better than most girls of her age with both parents did. LJ brought her an omelet made exactly how she wanted it. She sat with her feet cocked up on the couch, clutching the phone. "I love you baby, you take good ass care of us."

"You know I got us, baby." Kissing her forehead, LJ walked off into the bedroom to grab some clothes to go out in. Tyler wanted to have a brothers' night. They honestly hadn't spent that much time together. Ty was always with Cay, or driving back and forth out of town for product. LJ was busy with the team; being captain meant he had to keep everyone on their toes. After the season ended, they promised they would go and visit their mother together, something she and Mama Pearl would love. LJ heard Evie yell from the living room that her dad was on the phone and he smiled, loving her happiness.

"This is a collect call from an inmate, press one to accept." Evie immediately pressed the button on her touch screen phone.

"Hey baby girl, how's things on the outside?"

"Erything's good, Daddy, aren't you excited you're about to be a grandpa?"

She giggled as he smacked his lips. "Told you don't call me grandpa, girl, I'm still young and on fleek." Evie and her father talked for a good ten minutes; she told him she was having a boy. He was just as happy as she and LJ were. They talked about baby names and she really loved the name Messiah. She would have to run it by LJ, but anything she wanted, he would go for. "Baby, before this phone hang up, I got sumthin' real critical to tell you." Evie made sure to listen clearly, so he would not have to repeat himself and waste time. "LJ's dad is in here with me, he don't know if they know about him or not, but when you said his name, I instantly knew. His old man's a good dude; we keep each other alive in here." She could feel her eyes well up as the tears formed. This was as good a bit of news as them being pregnant was. LJ never knew what happened to his father, and this would make a huge difference.

"Oh my goodness, Daddy, that is hella good news, hopefully we can find a way to communicate with him. I know LJ's mom would love to know that." Just as Evie said that, the voice came over the phone warning them that they had one more minute to talk.

"Well, I love you, baby doll, be safe and send me pregnant belly pics."

"I love you, Pop, I definitely will, be safe and tell LJ's dad I said hey." The phone clicked off and Evie turned around to see LJ standing behind her with a blank stare on his face. "Damn baby, how long you been standing there? You scared me." She smiled, but he wasn't in a joking mood.

"Evie, what the fuck was that about?" She walked over to him, rubbing her belly, hoping he wouldn't get too upset.

"Baby, yo daddy is my dad's cellmate."

LJ could feel his head start spinning and everything went black. He didn't know if he was dreaming, because it felt so real. His father, Tyler, and his mother all sitting on a couch together. They were all in their current ages, happy and a family again. "Lee, baby, wake up, baby please, bae, please... you scarin' the fuck outta me." He could hear her voice, but his eyes didn't want to open.

"Baby, calm down; I'm okay, just got a lil dizzy." Rubbing his hand over his face, he rubbed his eyes vigorously. As the image of his family faded, LJ opened his eyes to see Evie sitting beside him. She had put a pillow underneath his head.

"Baby, what the hell?" She popped his chest after seeing he was okay.

"Sorry mami, I ain't mean to scare you, but did you say what I think you said?"

"Yeah baby, Daddy said he known yo dad for years and when I told him yo name, he just knew it was you, just like fate in a way." She helped him off the floor, into their bedroom. Evie began to give him a massage, helping him out of his shirt. "It's real good news ain't it baby, you can reach out to him and let him know about your mom. From what my dad says he would be happy to hear from you."

LJ smiled, so as not to upset his pregnant fiancée, but deep down, he didn't know how to feel about his father. All this time, how in the fuck was he in prison, and why had he never tried to reach out to them? On the other hand, he missed his family, and the few memories he has of his father were good ones. He wasn't even in Chicago a year yet, and so much shit was coming out of the woodworks.

"Baby, we gonna have to make plans to visit him and your dad." She hugged his neck tight, knowing he would do anything to make her happy. As far as his father went, he would just have to see how things went between the two of them. He would never be disrespectful, but he had questions that he wanted the answers to.

"So daddy, what are you wearing to your brother's lil strip party?" She folded her arms, looking at him through the mirror on their wall.

"Ma, it ain't no damn strip party, we just goin' out, having a few drinks and joints, no bitches. I promise." He leaned backward and kissed her forehead softly,

"Bet not be, nigga, I'll be in there barefoot, pregnant, and packin'." She imitated a shotgun with her hands, and he laughed at her.

"Vee, only thang you packin' is my baby and my last name, woman." Pulling him onto the bed, she climbed on top of him. "Damn, that pregnant woman strength." She laughed hard, biting his cheek.

"Nigga, if it was up to me, yo ass would be stayin' put, lucky it's Ty takin' you somewhere." Kissing her lips softly, he rubbed her ass.

"I love you, mami."

"I love you more, daddy." Evie grabbed some True Religion jeans and a green polo shirt. LJ tried it on, looking in the mirror as she stood behind him, rubbing her hands over his dick. "Gotta make sho' that dickprint ain't visible."

Turning around, he picked her off her feet, kissing her very slow, before sitting her on the bed. "I'll be home soon as the drinks hit my dick, bae, I promise."

"Don't play wit' me, nigga." Kissing her one last time, LJ made his way out the front door.

Tyler was waiting for him in his truck at the corner. "Nigga, you ready to get so fucked up you forget yo name?"

Thinking of the current events that had taken place that sounded like a good ass idea. "Shit bruh, let's go and do this shit, I'm too ready." They drove off into the night; it felt good to have someone to kick it with that you didn't have to watch your back around.

"So nigga how's everything with the baby?"

"Shit nigga, it's cool, except the late night cravings and mood swings, the sex is fuckin incredible; best pussy is pregnant pussy." They shook hands and laughed, pulling up to the first bar they saw.

"I'll be right there my nigga, know I gotta adjust the strap." LJ knew his brother meant fit his gun into his jacket, so he hopped out and walked up to the bouncer. Minutes later, Tyler walked up to LJ, but he wasn't alone. "LJ, shit ran into this old muhfucker walking from the car, aye bouncer, wat's good nigga? Yo, let us in."

LJ thought if he downed the shots, it would improve his attitude. All the liquor did was piss him off even more. Every time he looked at Jamal, he wanted to kill him. He wanted him to feel the pain that he and his mother felt all those years ago. "Bruh, you good nigga, you want anotha dance ah sumthin'?" LJ could tell that Tyler knew he wasn't feeling the situation and was trying to make him feel as comfortable as possible.

"Nah bruh, I'm good, matta fact, Evie just texted me she ain't feeling good. I'm 'bout ta bounce." Tyler nodded his head, he understood his brother hated Jamal and would give him time to adjust. He appreciated the fact that LJ didn't snap off on the man that raised him. Leaning over to Tyler, LJ whispered, "Lemme holla at you fa a second, bruh." The boys both walked outside, "Man, check this out, Evie's dad locked up and he told her today that my dad is his cell mate. Nigga, the shit been fuckin' wit' me, but I'ma holla at you in the morning before the game."

Tyler shook his brother's hand and pulled him close, hugging him. "Be strong bruh, I'm here if you need me." LJ drove home in silence; he still couldn't get the image of Jamal sitting smug, with a stripper on his lap, as if he had done nothing wrong at all. If it wasn't for the love he had for his brother, and the fact that he was about to have a family of his own, he would have put a bullet in his head the moment he saw him.

Walking into his apartment, the quiet was peaceful. Sneaking into his bedroom, he could hear Evie's low snoring. Kissing her check, he undressed himself before sliding into bed beside her with just his boxers on. Reaching over to turn his phone off, he noticed he had a missed message. It was from an anonymous number. Looking over to make sure Evie was still asleep he opened the message. "Nigga you ain't gotta like me, but yo young ass gon' respect me." He automatically knew it was from Jamal. Not all the love in the world was going to keep LJ from killing him now; he would apologize to his brother later.

CHAPTER 24

Leroy had spent the last twenty years of his life in prison. He never even had a trial or any kind of judgment. The white bastards threw him away like an old piece of trash; no one ever even questioned him just popping up. These last few months had been great, he had made some kind of contact with his son and now he was about to be a grandfather. LJ was around the same age as his father when he and Lisa had him. With the problems he had growing up, Leroy was proud of the way his son turned out. He couldn't wait to hug his son and grandchild, and lastly but definitely just as important, he had to see Lisa.

"Yo Gunn, ma nigga, real shit, good lookin' on the info, shit feel good to be getting old nah." Gunn was busy doing push-ups as Leroy paced the floor of their cell, talking about their kids.

"Lucky he got him a good girl like Evangeline; can't wait to be out this bitch, family."

"Hell yeah, bro, ma daughter gon' set me up wid a lil spot and help me get on ma feet. This shit here, ain't nun good 'bout it." Getting up, they got ready for lunchtime. "You need to put him on yo visitors' list folk, make sho' that lil nigga can come up here and see you."

Leroy nodded; he would make sure he did just that. Nothing would make him happier than seeing LJ in person; he knew he was going to bitch up and cry. Having not seen his son since he was only two and a half years old, he knew he would break down like a baby. "Shit, soon as I shove that shit they call food in my face, I'ma go talk to that bitch ass, Warden Stalls."

"Watch where the fuck you goin' old man." Leroy turned around to see a young man, around the same age as his son, with his face all frowned up and his chest poked out.

"Excuse me, lil nigga?" Leroy rubbed his chin, he hadn't been in the hole in a month, and he wanted to keep it that way.

"Yo, you fuckin' heard me, watch the fuck out." The boy stepped up to Leroy, but before he could grab the dude by the neck, Gunn stepped in between them.

"Yo lil nigga, trust and believe, this ain't what you want, ya hear me?" Gunn pressed his chest up against the boy's and stared into his eyes with an evil look.

"Ma bad, no disrespect, y'all excuse me." Turning to Leroy, Gunn pushed him over toward the wall. "Yo bro, we don't need to be getting in no shit the time is now to control yo tempa, you feel me?"

Leroy looked at the boy, who was sitting in a chair staring at them, talking shit under his breath. "Yeah ma bad, I feel you, folk." They sat down and ate, and the whole time, Leroy could feel the boy's eyes burning a hole into his back. Regardless of almost being forty, Leroy was always aware of his surroundings, no matter where he went. Leroy knew he didn't have to worry much; he and Gunn were a force to be reckoned with. He knew niggas that he would kill, just for looking at him funny. "Fuck is that lil nigga's prollem, fam?"

Gunn looked behind himself boldly, staring into the young dude's face. "Shit, I'on know but fuck his lil ass; long as he stays ova there." Leroy finished eating and shook hands with Gunn, letting him know that he would see him back in their cell. Shoving a piece of ham and cheese sandwich in his mouth, Gunn nodded his head, so Leroy could know he understood him. "Gotcha boss man."

Before he left the cafeteria, Leroy noticed that the young nigga that was talking all that shit had dipped off. He didn't care, as long as he could take care of business, he wasn't checking for where the fucker went. As LJ went to turn the corner, he didn't see any guards or other inmates in the halls. It was awkwardly quiet in the prison hallway. He didn't even see the little nigga jump out from behind a corner with a shank in his hand.

"You thought I was gon' let it go, muhfucka?" Leroy was confused; he knew this boy wasn't trying to kill him just because they'd bumped into one another.

"The fuck wrong wid you boy, young ass need help."
The boy walked up closer to Leroy as if he was going to
strike. "Nah bitch, I need ma father, but yo ass took him
away from me."

Before he had a chance to think about anything, he
felt the blade slice across his stomach. "Shit, you lil
muhfucka, look; I don't wanna hurt you, I don't 'een
know who the fuck you are." Swinging the blade again,
but this time Leroy dodged it as he wondered why in the
fuck no one was around.

"One night I was just playing in ma room, and all of
a sudden I hear a gunshot, my dad had always lemme
watch him shoot, so I knew exactly what it sounded like."
Leroy stood with his guard up and listened to the boy tell
his story. "I walked out to see my father lying dead, and
the police dragging yo ass out the front door. Yeah he did
illegal shit, but he had a fuckin' family. My mom's killed
herself after that shit, ma brother got locked up and
killed, and I knew the only way I'd be able to sleep good
at night was if I killed you."

Dodging at Leroy again, the boy wasn't expecting
what was about to happen. Leroy grabbed him, squeezing
his wrist until he dropped the shank to the floor.
Wrapping his arms around the boy's neck, Leroy
squeezed until the boy's body went limp. Checking his
pulse, he made sure he was still breathing. "Fuck this
shit… ain't happenin'." Just as he was done dragging the
boy's body back into the corner he'd jumped out of,

Leroy made his way to his cell. The time had passed for him to see the warden, and he knew he wasn't trying to go back to the hole for missing count. Sorry he couldn't say the same for the boy who just tried to kill him. Gunn was looking confused, Leroy didn't come from the way of the warden's office, and he could see the blood coming from his side and hands. Gunn stood up and cracked his neck, helping Leroy onto the bunk.

Putting his finger up to his lips, motioning for Gunn to keep his voice down, Leroy grabbed his sheet, ripping off a piece. He quickly told Gunn to help him wrap it around his stomach to stop the bleeding; he knew going to the infirmary meant they did an investigation. Those bitches couldn't even tell him why he was there; he never asked them for more than what they gave him. "Look, that lil nigga from the lunchroom, jumped me on my way to the warden's office. lil bitch think I killed his dad all them years ago, the shit I ain do the reason I'm in here. my so called best friend set me up, shit's crazy cause I shoulda killed him but I didn't, but when he wake up in the hole from having that shank, he gon' have time to rethink shit." Gunn wanted to go and finish the boy off, but Leroy assured him he wasn't a major threat. By the time he got out the hole, he was hoping to be gone and back on the outside.

"A'ight family, I'll take yo word fa it, fa now we just need to work on getting LJ on yo call and visiting list." The pain in his side was getting worse; he honestly didn't know how deep the cut was and didn't want to find out.

He didn't want any reason to have to go to the infirmary. Grabbing his side, he applied pressure to the wound.

"Shit, tomorrow ain't promised, but hopefully in the morning before breakfast, I can get ova there." Gunn checked to make sure that no guards were coming down that hallway and lit up a small joint for Leroy. The weed they got was never dro, as he was used to smoking, but it was good enough to get them blazed enough to forget reality. "Good lookin', ma nigga."

Leroy took a long drag from the joint, laying his head back against the cold concrete. If he bled out, he knew nothing would stop Gunn from killing that kid and anyone who got in his way. However, he had hope and faith, in the morning he would patch up his side and go talk to Stalls.

The next morning, Leroy could feel that the bed was different. Blinking his eyes repeatedly, they finally adjusted to the light; he tried to rise up, but his wrists were handcuffed to the bed. "Fuck, yo what the fuck is goin' on?"

A tall, cute, dark-skinned nurse walked over to him and checked his vital readings on the monitor's screen. "Sir, your best bet is to remain calm and you won't have to be in psych that long." He looked around, noticed a bunch of crazy looking, fidgety inmates, he wanted to scream; this is one place he never wanted to be. Psych was a place for niggas that went off the deep far deep end.

"Nurse, I don't belong here, I need to get back to my cell." Jerking his arm, he tried to yank the handcuff off the bed railing.

"It's no use, you're weak from the drugs and sir, you won't be able to leave until they think you are no longer suicidal." Leroy had no idea what she was talking about, and then he reached his free hand over to his wounded side. It was all bandaged up, and he couldn't even feel it anymore. He figured it was the drugs; it felt good that they doped him up with the good stuff, but it sucked that he was surrounded by psychos. "Once the medicine wears off, you will be able to eat, but you still have to be confined to that bed. Mr. Burman, are you listening?"

Leroy was staring out of the window of the small doctor's office, and he saw them dragging the boy off towards the hole. Gunn knew the only thing that could keep his mind off killing the young boy was to workout. Through the night Leroy had begun to bleed more; it had even made a puddle underneath the bed. He had tried to wake him up and when he got no response, he knew he had to get the guard. Gunn decided to make up a story about Leroy trying to kill himself over missing his wife and son; it was hard making them understand why he chose to cut his side, but the guards believed it nevertheless. He hoped his homie would live to see their grandchild.

––––––––––––

"Baby, have you seen my wallet, it was 'posed to be in yo truck?" Caymalia walked around the house nervously, she had to hurry up and get to the store. Her monthly visitor skipped her last month, and she didn't know what to say to Tyler. She wasn't going to tell him that she might be pregnant, that would start a big ass fight. Then she thought about how the last few weeks, they had been closer than ever. He told her that he loved her just as much as she wanted.

"Nah baby, but what you need all you gotta do is ask, daddy got you." She smiled at how sweet he was, maybe he wouldn't freak out if she told him. "Just a few dollas fa some personal things, baby, or I can just go to Peaches, can you drop me off?"

Tyler walked from the bathroom, brushing his teeth with a towel wrapped around his waist. "I can take you to da sto' mami, I ain't got shit to do." Kissing him on his long neck, Caymalia rubbed his dick through the towel. "Yo ass betta stop it, or you won't be goin nowhere but in that room."

Giggling, she walked into the bedroom, grabbing her sneakers. Tyler watched her juicy ass sway as she walked away from him. Every time she walked it bounced, she made her ass wiggle on purpose because she knew he was watching. He hadn't talked to his father since he'd told him that stupid shit about Caymalia. His father never gave him a reason to doubt his word, but this time just had to be different. Jamal couldn't be Caymalia's father.

Wouldn't it be fucked up if they had kids and they came out deformed, because he couldn't listen? Pushing it deep in the back of his mind was working at first, but some things she did reminded him of himself. Maybe it was because of all the time they spent together.

"I love you, Killa."

"I love you, Cay baby." Either way, at this very moment he didn't care; that girl worshiped the ground he walked on. She would do whatever he wanted and never asked questions. What more could he ask for?

CHAPTER 25

Never having to buy a pregnancy test before, Caymalia was completely lost walking around the store. She had to keep looking over her shoulder to make sure that Tyler didn't come inside. Not knowing how he would feel about the current situation, she would rather find out by herself, and then figure out what to do. Watching him tap his fingers on the steering wheel, she felt as if she was betraying him, because they were in a relationship, but she would have no relationship if he wasn't feeling her having his baby. Looking at the labels, she noticed the name of a few she had seen on commercials. Grabbing the most expensive one, she knew she had to hurry up and get it over with. Hopping back into the truck with Tyler, Cay has a smug look on her face. Tyler had just shoved his phone into his pocket as if he was trying to hide something. "What's wrong, ma?"

She didn't even hide her feelings. "Who was on the phone?"

He could tell she had seen him; he didn't want to answer Jamal's calls, and he didn't want to tell her he was ignoring him, because she would want to know why.

"Baby, that was just business; calm down damn." She wanted to believe him, but all she could think about was some bitch trying to take her place. "I hear you, baby, let's get home so we don't miss my TV show." She smiled and he leaned over and kissed her cheek softly.

"So you get what you needed, bae?" Tyler adjusted the radio, and Fetty Wap's "Trap Queen" blared through the speakers.

"Yeah love, I got erything I need and want." Looking in her eyes, he could see how happy she was. Before her, his heart was ice cold, her love and care seemed to warm his heart in more ways then one.

"Babymama, you feelin okay or nah?" Evie was finally in the final month of her pregnancy, and she was wobbling around the house like a drunk penguin.

"Stop callin' me that, dammit, and yeah baby, I'm feelin' okay, wish yo damn son would stop kickin me." LJ laughed, he loved watching her walk around barefoot and pregnant.

"I'm finna hop in the shower, lemme know if you need me to get anything sexy thickness." Smacking her on the ass, LJ started the shower. Before he could get his shorts off, he heard Evie yelling. Trying not to fall, he rushed from the bathroom. "Baby shit, what's wrong, erything okay?" She was leaning against the hallway wall, with fluid running down her inner thighs. "Damn baby, why you pissin' on the floor?"

She pushed him in the chest. "Fucker, my water broke; I'm goin' into labor."

"Oh shit, baby, stay put I'ma call the midwife." Evie always wanted to have a home water birth; LJ bought everything she needed to make her dream birth come true. She wanted it to be an all-natural birth; he kept insisting she take an epidural. Evie refused to bring her baby into the world all doped up. After filling the tub with lukewarm water, LJ helped his fiancée out of her t-shirt and into the water carefully. "Shit baby, is she here yet?" Rubbing her shoulders, and kissing her forehead, LJ reassured her to remember her breathing exercises and that the midwife would be there shortly.

They heard the front door swing open, and a short, stubby lady waddled into the room. "How's she doin', Lee?" She had an adorable high voice, something you'd like, but wouldn't want to hear all the time.

"They 'bout five minutes apart, but she pissed off; she keep cussin' me out and I ain't 'een do nun." LJ shook his head, and the midwife Lucinda just laughed.

"Oh love, that's just the labor pains, you gon' be a few mo' muhfuckers before this is all over."

"Oooh fuck... LJ, get the fuck back in here." He reached out to her as she grabbed his hand, squeezing it tight. "I'm here fa you baby, I love you."

"Ohh LJ... I fuckin' hate you, you did this shit to me, fucker."

Smiling, he kissed her cheek, rubbing her forehead. "I love you more, baby, nah the midwife is gon' take good care of you and Alarik." Evie had let her father pick their son's name. She and LJ kept getting stumped; they loved what Gunn came up with and it meant ruler of all, a proper name for their baby.

"Okay my lovely, breathe for me, now on three, I want you to push, okay baby?" While Lucinda held the back of Evie's head and LJ held her hand tight, she let out a loud groan and then a yelp as she pushed one long hard time.

Rubbing her stomach, LJ kissed Evie's cheek repeatedly. "You doin' good, ma, just keep breathin'." He could hear her whispering how much she loved him; he smiled as Lucinda checked for the baby's head. "Oh my goodness, lil sucker has a head full of hair." LJ peeked down between her legs, and saw a bushel of wet curly hair. He honestly he thought that the sight would make him pass out, but he actually loved seeing her give birth up close and personal. "Shit baby, look at our boy, hell yeah." LJ was more excited than Evie was.

"Okay, just a little more darling; keep breathing like I showed you." Evie laid her head to the side, gripping LJ's hand even tighter, and began to push. She screamed even louder, digging her nails into LJ's skin. After a long hard push, and fifteen minutes of labor, Alarik was crying loudly in Evie's arms. One look at him and she began crying, their son was more beautiful than anything she had ever seen.

LJ grabbed his phone, taking a picture of his newborn son and soon-to-be wife. He could feel one single tear fall down his face. Never in his mind did he think he would ever be that happy. After draining the birthing tub, LJ helped the midwife pack up all of her accessories. Evie was lying on the couch with the baby; he was all bundled up in his blue blanket. They had found him a lot of stuff with crowns on it online. After telling her that she didn't have a price limit, Evie went bananas ordering shit for the baby. He leaned over and kissed her softly on the forehead, after hearing the door shut. "You did good, baby, I fuckin' love you."

She raised her head up, cuddling the baby closer, and kissed him. "I love you more daddy, you mean we did good." He wished she could come to his game tomorrow, but he knew she had to heal. LJ would make sure he kicked ass and dedicated the game to son and Evie.

LJ slept on the floor, right under Evie and the baby. He wanted her to move to the bedroom, but she had fallen asleep by the time he got everything ready. He just made himself a pallet on the floor, making sure not to wake her and the baby. The sun shone bright through the window, Evie still slept peacefully with their baby boy in her arms. He was a sweet and quiet baby, only made a few noises since he was born less than twenty-four hours ago. LJ was lucky to have them both in his life. He wanted to wake them up, but she needed her rest. Quickly scribbling his whereabouts on a piece of paper, LJ put it where he knew she would find it and made his way to the gym for their first championship game in years.

Tyler promised that he would show up and that he wouldn't bring Jamal. Seeing him would just piss Jamal off and throw his head off the game. That's something he didn't need. An hour into practice, his cell phone rang. Evie woke up and wanted to wish him good luck. Hearing her voice and the baby cooing in the background was a warming feeling. With the stadium starting to fill up, LJ saw Tyler walking with his arm wrapped tightly around Caymalia. After shaking half of the people's hands, he finally made it over to his big brother. "Sup ma nigga, you finna kick some ass in here or what?"

LJ grinned, pulling his brother into a shoulder hug. "Nigga it's pig pussy pork. Holla if ya hear me." They laughed as the buzzer went off for the game to begin. As usual, LJ had Evie on his mind, but now he had another person to play for. He wanted always to make sure his son wanted for nothing. To secure the future he saw for his family, he knew he had to give basketball all he had. After his teammate smacked the ball his way, LJ dribbled fast, making his way to the rim as quickly as possible. Whizzing past three players, he glided up towards the rim, making a lay-up. The crowd roared his name, yelling his number as they always did. LJ as always, stole the show.

Tyler walked up to his brother after the crazy fans finally disbursed from around him. "Nigga, wish I woulda bet on yo ass, you need to be in the NBA fa real." The brothers hugged as Caymalia congratulated her "brother-in-law" before heading to the truck.

"Nigga, I know I'ma make it; can't stay here fa eva."

Tyler smiled a little, and then put his head down, he wished that he felt that way, but he loved the place where he was the prince. "Bruh, how 'bout I let Cay take da truck and we walk to da bar?"

LJ could text Evie; she wouldn't mind him spending a few hours with his brother. "Hell yeah, fam, lead the way." Evie texted back that she was cool with him staying out, she was happy that they won the trophy. After the year they had, he planned to lie up under her and Alarik for the whole winter.

"So bruh, like how you and Jamal get along?" Since the Cay thing, Tyler didn't even think about his father that much, but he knew he would have to speak to him sooner than later.

"Shit, we cool when we coo,l and when we bad, we just stay out each other's way."

"That's wasup, bruh; I'm sorry we don't get along, I know it bother you."

Tyler downed another shot of Hennessy. "Shit bruh, erybody got issues, I ain't rushin fa you and the nigga ta be friends, we all grown." LJ could see that his brother was getting a little faded and insisted they cut it for the evening. "One mo' bruh, toast to family, fam." LJ lifted the last shot glass, as the boys tilted their heads back at the same time. "I love you, fam."

"Love you mo' lil bruh." They walked, hanging on one another's shoulders, as they did when they first met.

"Damn, can't buhlee I'ma uncle, bruh, yo ass finna start getting gray hair and shit." LJ laughed as they sat down on Tyler's porch, the light was off. Caymalia must have been asleep. "Bruh, nigga, just glad I ain't have a girl."

"Hell yeah, nigga, I ain't fa dat twerking shit, dat's dead." Tyler leaned back, laying his head on the concrete step, as his brother handed him a joint. A few minutes of silence went by and a car pulled up in front of them.

The music was blasting so loud that the plants on the stoop shook; after the engine stopped running, Tyler lifted his drunken head. "Damn, it's Mal; uh, you wanna wait in there you can, bruh."

"Nah ma nigga, I'ma bounce, hit me up lata tho." Before LJ could get too far down the street, he had stopped. Jamal was yelling so loudly at Tyler that it pissed him off a little. "Nigga, I'on give a fuck what go on, yo ass don't ignore ma calls." Tyler could see that his brother was worried, and waved him off, but LJ wouldn't budge.

"Nigga, you ain't gotta disrespect me, especially dis muhfuckin' late, I hear you." Jamal started to poke Tyler in the chest, if he wasn't drunk, he was gonna wish he was.

"Aye bruh, you ain't gotta put yo hands on my brotha."

Turning to LJ, Jamal had a screwed up look on his face. "The fuck you talkin to, nigga? I raised him, bitch ass nigga, you don't run shit, so you betta watch yoself." Before he could catch himself, LJ shoved Jamal into his own truck.

"Lee, let him alone, man, just fuck it, bruh. He ain't worth it, man, think 'bout Evie and Alarik." Tyler held onto LJ's arm,

Jamal straightened out his clothes, laughing in his face. "Yeah nigga, definitely ain't worth it, mind yo own fuckin' business."

LJ looked into his brother's eyes; he could tell his brother was praying he'd let the whole thing go. "Love you lil bruh."

"Love you too, fam." As he walked off, he could still hear Jamal yelling at Tyler. That night, his plan was to go home, kiss his wife-to-be, hold his beautiful son, and take care of the fucked up problem—Jamal.

"LJ, where have you been?" Evie walked up to LJ with the baby's bottle in her hand.

"Chilling bae, what happen to the tiddy suckin'?" They both laughed.

"They hurt and tenda as fuck, baby, gon' try lil man on the bottle and see how he like it."

"Well, I know he smart like his daddy, baby boy gon' love dem tiddys." He grabbed her, kissing her lips softly, sucking her bottom lip into his mouth. "You so damn beautiful, my Evangeline." Maybe he was risking too much by wanting to kill Jamal.

CHAPTER 26

The next morning was hell; he hadn't talked to Caymalia in hours and knew she would be tripping.

"Nigga, you got a lot of fuckin' explainin' to do, nah yo ass done sobered up, and you betta properly check yo brotha, or I will."

Tyler rubbed his temples; he had a bad hangover and needed something to eat. "Look Mal, I feel you on me disappearin' and shit, but I needed time to think 'bout shit. I love Cay and I ain't lettin' her go, you said yoself; her moms was a hoe, don't 'een know why you brought that shit up."

Jamal had lit a cigar, leaning back in his recliner chair. "Nigga, 'cause you fuckin' needed to know, felt betta getting that shit off ma chest, I was shitty to her moms and shit; that was something like closure." Shaking his head, Tyler stood up, he didn't need this shit.

"The fuck are you goin', lil nigga?"

"Got some shit to handle."

Getting up and grabbing a duffle bag from his closet, Jamal tossed it at Tyler's feet. "Take care of that shit while you out, and make sho' nigga if I call, you betta answer, hear me?"

Rolling his eyes, he nodded his head and walked out the front door. Checking his phone, he had a few missed calls, and about ten messages. Cay and his brother had seemed to be tag teaming his phone; he felt glad that they were worried about his well-being. Well, at least LJ was, Cay was going to try to wring his neck for not coming home or calling.

"Baby girl, before you trip, I can explain."

Caymalia was sitting on the couch, with her knees up to her chest. "Bae, come sit down for a minutes, now." He walked over as fast as he could, no reason to make her more upset then she was.

"What's wrong, mami?" Pulling her hands from between her legs, Cay laid her head on Tyler's shoulder. Grabbing his hand, she laid something in his palm. As he looked down, he saw a pregnancy test. "Baby, is this what I think this is?"

For a moment, she thought he was upset, and then he pulled her close and tight, kissing her cheek and neck repeatedly. "Baby, you not mad?"

Rubbing her cheek, Tyler could see that she was crying. "Ma, hell nah I ain't mad, you ma baby; I'm happy as fuck." She wrapped her arms around his neck, pulling him closer, sucking his tongue into her mouth. "I love you, papi."

"I love you, mami."

Hugging her close and tight, Tyler laid the pee stick on her lap. "Eww baby; forgot you peed on that." He rubbed his hand on her thigh as she laughed. Tyler explained he had to make a run, but he would be back before nightfall.

"Be safe, daddy." Leaving the apartment, Tyler was happy; he immediately texted his brother, telling him the great news. LJ let him know how happy he was for him, and that many things would change when he became a father. As much as he appreciated all his father had done, Tyler wasn't planning to deal forever. The deal he had to do was with some local white boys. They threw huge ass parties and did so much blow that they couldn't think straight, but they always paid good and upfront. When he got there, the whole place was dark. No one was in sight; Tyler grabbed his gun from underneath his shirt. "Aye, the fuck y'all at, I know Mal called."

He heard rustling behind him; he turned around as he aimed his gun at the man's face. "Be cool, homie, everything good, just be calm." Tyler clutched the bag as he followed the tall, fat man through the house. "The fuck is my money man, I ain't got all day." As the got into the family room, Tyler watched the man reach into a tote on the floor. Instead of Tyler's money, he pulled out a shotgun and aimed it at Tyler's chest. "Fuck, y'all don't know who you fuckin' wit'."

Cocking the gun, the man smiled at Tyler. "Actually, I do."

Before the man could walk any closer, Tyler pulled the trigger, shooting him directly between the eyes. "Told you muhfucka, you didn't." Grabbing the money and the guns, Tyler walked back to his truck. Shit had never gone that way before, it was damn peculiar all of a sudden that they'd try to jack him. He had to talk to Mal about this shit.

Evie had gone to visit her aunt in downtown Chicago, so LJ figured this would be the perfect time to have that long overdue, heart to heart with Jamal. He hadn't planned anything; he honestly didn't know how the shit would end, but he knew one thing; Jamal was going to listen to every word he had to say. "I love you, baby, be safe and kiss our king for me." Evie blew a kiss through the phone.

"We love you more, daddy." She would be back in the morning; he hoped to be home way before that. Tyler had texted him some good news about a baby coming soon. Even though he didn't think Tyler was mentally stable, he was glad and proud that his brother was happy and accepting his seed. After making sure that he still had the gun Tyler gave him, LJ set off for his destination. Having never actually been to Jamal's place, LJ had no idea where he was going, but he knew exactly how to find what he was looking for. Walking down the street, he just waited to see a fiend, which wasn't hard in Chicago in the afternoon, fiends came out at night for real. "Hey daddy, you looking for a good time?" On his left stood an overweight, extra black prostitute with a bleach blonde wig on.

"Nah ma, but I got a business proposition for you."

She smiled, showing a set of rotten teeth; LJ tried not to gag. "What can I do ya for?" Leaning against the alley wall, he made sure not to be seen. Reaching into his pocket, he pulled out a wad of money. After pulling off two hundred-dollar bills, LJ slid them into her clearly visible push up bra.

"You know where King Mal stay?"

She smacked her lips, looking him up and down. "You a fuckin' cop, ain't you?" Before she could storm off, he grabbed her by the forearm, pulling another bill from his pocket.

"I ain't no damn police, so don't run from me again."

Straightening out her skirt, she looked into his eyes. "The king has a few houses and shit, but traps on Christiana Street, around this time. He should be standing outside wid his boys." Shaking his head with approval, LJ let go of the lady, walking off into the shadows.

He knew driving up to his front door was out of the question, so LJ decided to walk. Hoping to see Jamal standing outside, or even in his truck would do. LJ wanted him to feel the same pain that he felt after losing Tyler, and even though she wasn't dead, he felt that he'd lost his mother. Getting closer to the street corner, LJ saw a bunch of men in black hoods. None of them seemed to be Jamal, so LJ walked past them as fast as he could without drawing any attention. "Sup fool, you need something?" They thought he was a basehead.

"Nah fam, I'm Gucci."

Without looking up, LJ strolled closer to the house where the chick said Jamal would be. The lights were on inside the house, and he could hear Jamal yelling at someone on the phone. "Muhfucka, you fucked up, so yo ass betta leave town, gotta do shit on my own roun' this bitch." Jamal threw the phone at the wall.

LJ found a side window with a perfect view of the room Jamal was in. A few minutes passed of Mal pacing the floor, and then a Mexican guy walks into the room. "Aye bro, shit ain't lookin' good with Hector; can we take him to the hospital?"

Jamal looked over at the man's face, "Muhfucka, y'all fucked it up, y'all fix it, drop that nigga off and get back here."

"But, Mal, homie, he's my little brother, I can't just leave him." The man's face turned from worried to terrified as Jamal walked toward him.

"Bitch, but nothing, the fuck outta here. If you stay wid him, make sho' yo ass don't come back ya feel me?" The man walked out and slammed Jamal's door, a few minutes later, a car was speeding down the street. Jamal laid back in his recliner chair; after turning on his music, he lit a fat blunt. LJ watched for about five minutes as Jamal enjoyed the last few puffs of the blunt. Tired of waiting, LJ noticed the front door was cracked and made his way inside the house. He honestly expected Mal to have security, but to his surprise, there was no one else inside. Making sure not to make too much noise with his feet, LJ stood in the doorway of Jamal's office. The house was huge, so he was glad he didn't have to play find the room. Lifting the gun, LJ aimed it at Jamal's head. "Damn nigga, you just gon' kill a nigga when his back turned?"

LJ had no clue how he knew he was there, but that wouldn't change what he was about to do. Jamal got up, taking off his t-shirt, revealing his pistol on his waist. "So you ain't got shit to say to me, lil Lee?" Hearing Jamal call him that just pissed him off even more, and LJ felt his finger tighten on the trigger.

"You fucked up my family, nigga; my mom's basically a damn vegetable 'cause of you, my brotha's a damn thug, you ain't shit for takin' him yo." Rubbing his chin, Jamal laughed at LJ.

"Nigga, yo moms was fucked up way before I came into the picture, as I recall she been crazy since yo daddy left." LJ had heard enough about his family from this home wrecking asshole.

"I tried to give it a chance for my brother's sake, but yo ass... just ain't no getting through to you that you the fuckin' problem."

"Yo ass ain't got the guts, you just like yo daddy." Before LJ could stop himself or change his mind, he lowered the gun and pulled the trigger.

The music was very loud, but he could hear Jamal screaming. "You son of a bitch, I'ma kill yo hoe ass." Before he could grab the pistol from his waist, LJ put another bullet into Jamal's other leg.

"See the difference between me and my daddy, bitch..." LJ smacked Jamal across the face with the hot revolver. "...I ain't him, muhfucka." LJ pressed down on the bullet hole in Jamal's leg. "I wonder do yo bitch ass have anything smart to say nah." Laughing, LJ stood up, staring down at Jamal as he cursed and clutched his legs.

"Yo ass betta kill me, nigga, or you ain't gon' never see that fuckin' bitch of yours again." Jamal had a demonic look in his eyes, but it was nothing, compared to the fire that had built up inside of LJ.

"Just tell me why man, why the fuck you take my brother and put my mama through all this shit?" At first, Jamal was going to tell LJ to fuck off, but he figured he was about to die anyway. "Fuck it, yo daddy stole my life and yo mama ain't want me and then she was gon' just take Ty away from me for good. Fucked up how I was gon' have to end up lonely, all she had to do was love me and it woulda been cool."

Shaking his head, LJ walked toward the doorway. Underneath Jamal, a pool of blood had formed; LJ figured he would bleed out sooner than later. "Well, yo ass is alone, 'cause my brother don't fuck wid you no mo, so just bleed and die, bitch."

Before LJ could get fully out of the house, Jamal yelled after him. "Bitch, if you don't kill me, you betta hope I do die, or I'ma fuck that bitch of yours and kill yo son, muhfucka. I don't grant mercy."

LJ walked back into the room and put the gun right in between Jamal's eyes, "Fuck you and yo mercy, bitch." After pulling the trigger, LJ felt the blood and brain matter spray onto his face. He could feel the thick tissue on his forehead and mouth. Swallowing the puke back down into his stomach, LJ walked as fast as he could away from that side of town. With the full on adrenaline rush he was feeling, he didn't even hear his phone ring the first time.

"Hey bruh, what's good?" Tyler was on the other end of the line; he sounded as if he was having problems.

LJ wondered if he had arrived right after he left and found Jamal. He had to play it as cool as possible. "Nigga, I need yo to meet me, some niggas just tried to kill me, bruh."

LJ could feel his heart drop into his stomach as he quickened his pace toward his apartment to get his truck. "The fuck you at, fam?"

"I'm headin' to Jamal's, think he tried to set me up or something man, shit don't feel right."

LJ tried to wrap his head around the whole situation; *maybe that's what Jamal was on the phone yelling about.* Now he really felt good about killing Jamal. "Text me the info, bruh, will be on my way." LJ would make sure his brother felt safe around him, he would even comfort him when they found Jamal's mangled body. After driving around for a few minutes, he finally pulled up beside Tyler's truck in front of Jamal's house. The police were everywhere, and the coroner's truck was parked at the corner. Tyler came out of the house with Caymalia's arms around his neck as tears flowed from his face. "What's wrong, Ty?" LJ tried to look as genuinely concerned as possible.

CHAPTER 27

Pulling Tyler into his arms, LJ scanned the scene to see if anyone was looking at him funny. "My dad dead, bruh, somebody shot him in the face. Yo, on my unborn, on Mama, bruh, when I find out who did this shit, I'm killin' 'em."

LJ felt confused, honestly after finding out Jamal could have set him up; he wasn't going to tell his little brother what he did. "What 'bout dat shit wid da Mexicans, bro?" Tyler sat on the curb; Caymalia went to roll him a joint for his nerves.

"Fam, I know you ain't like dude, but he raised me, showed me hella love and made sho' I handled everything like a man, even with our differences I ain't gon' eva turn ma back in him, especially nah." LJ shook his head, he understood, because if it were him, he would do the same thing. However, he didn't know how to make his brother understand what he did was justified.

"Damn, I gotta call Evie; I'll be back in a minute, bruh." Tyler put his face in his hands, trying to conceal his tears. "Dang baby, give him my condolences, and your bad ass son is doing good, greedy just like you, but we miss you, baby, can't wait to be home."

"I miss y'all more, baby, can't wait to see y'all." A part of him wished he could take it back, but then again, Jamal was the reason he grew up fatherless, at least Tyler was raised by Jamal. "Bruh, I'm finna hit the streets and see if I can find out anything. I'ma let you know and please don't try to stop me, that's why Cay left. I just need to do this." After hugging his brother, LJ went his own way. He would let his brother do his shit, and make sure he didn't get back to him, no matter what.

It had been a whole month, but to Tyler, it felt like only yesterday. He took his father's murder hard, even harder when the police said they couldn't do anything. They hated his father for all of his unanswered crimes, so when he died, to them that was a victory. Tyler had yet to find anything connected to his father's death. Everyone that visited his father that night had been thoroughly questioned the only way Tyler knew how. Matter of fact, he had one more person to talk to before he called it a night.

Caymalia walked out of the bathroom, her small round belly poking out from under her crop top. "Yo baby makin' my ankles swell."

He grabbed her, kissing her lips softly, rubbing her ass. "Sexy, swole ass ankles, baby."

She grabbed a bag of chips from the nightstand, seeing Tyler still dressed and it was almost midnight bothered her. "So bae, where you goin?" She always got straight to the point.

"Just gotta make one mo' run, baby, shit changed since I'm da king."

Caymalia stuck her tongue out and he grabbed it, pulling her close. "Daddy promise, I'ma be home to rub yo stomach and feed you ice cream."

Smiling, she hugged him around the neck tight. "Be careful, baby daddy."

The Mexicans was always cool with his dad, but that night, the shit that happened with him, he didn't put it past anyone. Approaching the building, he could see the lights on; he'd had his goons grab Pepe. Even though he was old school as fuck, Pepe still loved how all this new technology was taking over the world. The motherfucker recorded everything and anything. He was already fucked up, but Tyler hadn't had a chance to talk to him yet.

"So nigga, exactly what did you hear on the night my father died and you bet not forget shit." As he said this, Tyler pulled a leather case from his inner jacket pocket, as he unraveled it, inside were three sharp blades. "Do you need a little convincing, or do you think yo memory is just fine?"

Before Tyler could step any closer, the man started to cry. "Shit papi, I heard a prostitute telling somebody where ya pops stayed, don't know who it was or why, but they paid in cash." Grinning, Tyler grabbed the longest blade and quickly swiped it across Pepe's throat. That was the best news he had gotten in a while.

Tyler knew exactly who could help him find out who was working that night. That was the benefit of having hoes at your beck and call. "Peaches get yo ass ova here now, and don't forget to bring mighty mouth with you, a'ight?" Before she could answer, he hung up in her face, but he knew she still would come and tell him whatever he wanted to know for a sack. Opening the door for her, he pulled her inside. "Who got some extra money from a john the night Pop died?"

She rolled her eyes, walking over to the couch. "Damn, can a bitch get a hi or somethin'?"

Tyler grabbed her by the throat, slamming her up against the wall. "Bitch, don't fuckin' play wid me, nah who all had some extra that night, speak the fuck up." As he removed his hands from her throat, her body slumped to the floor.

"Fuck Killa, that shit fuckin' hurt, I'm sorry. Look, Caprice had a few extra hundreds from some nigga askin' questions." She reached her hand out, hoping he would help her up, but he smacked her hand away.

"What kinda fuckin' questions?" Rubbing her throat, she slid up the wall. "She never said, just got all happy and strolled off."

Tyler grabbed a bag from the table and tossed it at her feet, "A'ight get the fuck outta here." Snatching the bag from the ground, she ran out the front door.

"Aye baby, I might be a lil late, but I love you." He'd sent Caymalia a voice message and turned his phone off; he was about to take a trip on the hoe stroll. Being the girlfriend and baby mama of the king of Chicago had its perks, and then it had its bad moments. Listening to the message, she quickly tried to call his phone back, but she knew his routine. Cay tried her best not to think negatively, but he had a crazy ass hold on her. Rubbing her belly and eating her macadamia nut ice cream, she sat and watched old music videos; she would just wait up for her man.

The sun was rising and Evie had called and decided to stay another night, so her aunt could talk to Gunn. He had almost forgotten about her call today, not having her around for two whole days was freaking him out. Good thing he was keeping himself busy. "A'ight baby you betta not make me come kidnap y'all and bring y'all back." Evie laughed and blew him a kiss into the phone as she always did when she was away from him.

Tyler had called and told him about the progress he had made, so before something happened, he had to take care of that hooker problem. Heading back toward Christiana Street, LJ looked for the hooker he ran into that night. Thankfully, she was getting out of a van and walking off into the alley. At first, LJ just wanted to talk to her, but then he figured that would only, have her wanting more money. Sneaking up behind her, he grabbed her by the neck and squeezed hard and tight. Never in his life did he think he would be doing something like this, but he had a life and wanted to keep it the way it was. She fought, kicked and screamed, but it didn't help. LJ was big and strong enough to pull her beside a dumpster, someone walked past and to them; it just looked like they were fucking. As she drew her last breath, LJ laid her body against the dumpster and walked off the other way.

About an hour later, Tyler was walking down the sidewalk looking for the hooker they called Caprice. Everyone knew she was a lousy lay, but the head was stupendous. "Where Caprice at?" All eyes were on him, every girl out there knew him, and wanted to fuck him.

"Hey daddy, she dipped off around the corner wid some light skin hottie." After nodding his head, Tyler began to walk around the corner through the alley. The girls blew kisses and cooed at him, but his mind was nowhere near on pussy. Looking down the alley, Tyler could see a pair of legs sticking from behind the dumpster. The heels let him know that it was a hooker.

"Aye shorty, lemme holla at you fa a minute," he yelled, but didn't get an answer; he figured she had nodded off for a little nap and kicked her foot. "Aye ma, get up." Tyler knew exactly what had happened once her body slumped over to the side; her eyes were dead and lifeless looking. Bitch didn't smell bad, so it must have just happened, and looking around, he could see where she was attacked. Tyler was starting to think that someone didn't want him to know about what happened to Jamal. After the police, ambulance, and coroner left the scene, Tyler looked over it one more time. On the ground under some leaves was something shiny, at first, he thought his eyes were playing tricks on him. It was a basketball pendant. Just like the ones that you get in college. Tyler's body got hot; he automatically thought of his brother, but he didn't want to jump to that conclusion, but how could he not? LJ hated Jamal for what he did, taking Tyler all those years ago, but could he actually be capable of doing something like this? Maybe it was an old pendant, either way; he knew his brother would have a good explanation. Better yet, he'd better have a good explanation.

Tyler quickly grabbed his phone and texted his big brother to meet him at the bar they'd drank at when they first met up again, after all those years. In his head, he played the situation repeatedly. How could he approach his brother and accuse him of something like that? Then again, LJ had just as much motive as anyone else that hated Mal. Receiving LJ's message that he would be there, Tyler hopped in his truck and drove as fast and calm as possible. He could see LJ's truck and after parking, he had to hit a joint just to ease his nerves, and his trigger finger.

LJ had ordered a few shots of Hennessy to ease his nerves; from the sound of Tyler's voice on the phone, he had something to get off his chest. After throwing back the fourth shot, LJ noticed his brother walk in; he also noticed he kept his hand on his waist where his gun was. "Sup my lil nigga?"

Tyler bore the signs of a man that hadn't gotten proper sleep. LJ knew he would feel the same way if his father had been killed. "Shit, just need a few drinks, a nigga goin' through it." The bartender handed them the bottle at their request.

"You know I'm here fa you, bruh, I'ma good listener when I'm lit." Smiling, Tyler stared at the shiny pins on his brother's jacket, remembering the one he picked up where Caprice was killed; he noticed one was missing from the pattern on the sleeve. "So bruh, what's up wid dem glistenin' ass pendants?"

LJ tipped the bottle upward, wiping liquor from his chin. "Got one fa every year I played since elementary til nah."

Slipping his hand sneakily inside his pocket, Tyler stared down into his hand and compared the pins. It was for sure the same one; he tried not to change his facial expression, but he was beyond pissed off. LJ just sat there as if nothing was wrong, maybe it was the alcohol, or maybe it was actually he was cold hearted. He honestly he hated having these thoughts about his big brother, but he didn't grow up with him, so he didn't really know what he was capable of.

LJ had no idea his brother suspected him. "So anybody know who did Mal?"

Tyler felt a sharp pain shoot through his head and neck, his body got hot for a minute and he felt as if his blood was boiling. "Shit nothing yet, but something bound to come up muhfuckas can't hide foreva, ya feel me?"

LJ felt the hair on his neck rise; turning to his brother, he could see the pain in his eyes. "Yeah, I feel you, youngin'." The boys were good and drunk, lying in a booth in the bar. Tyler watched as his brother tried to balance a bottle on the edge of the couch. Looking down, he could see some dark sticky shit on LJ's jeans. The same shit was on the side of the dumpster where he found the hooker earlier; he wondered what the fuck was up with LJ. Tyler didn't know what was going on, but one thing was for sure, if LJ had anything to do with killing Jamal, Evie was going to be a single parent.

To Be Continued...

Join our mailing list to get a notification when Leo Sullivan Presents has another release!

Text LEOSULLIVAN to 22828 to join!

To submit a manuscript for our review, email us at leosullivanpresents@gmail.com

Coming Soon from Sullivan Productions!

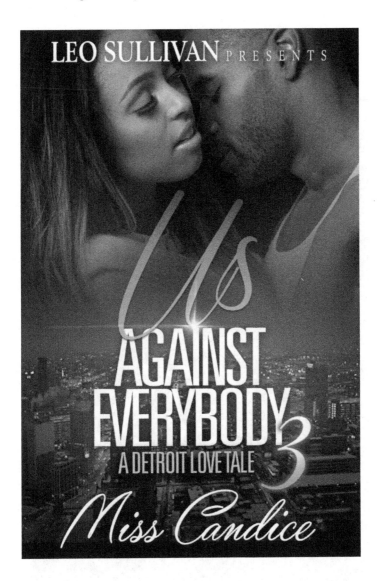

A Thug's Betrayal   Sativa Outlaw

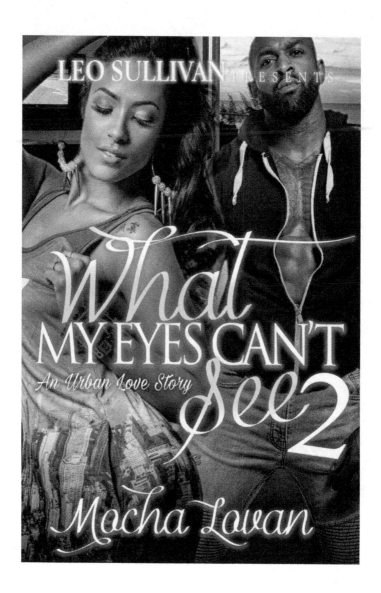

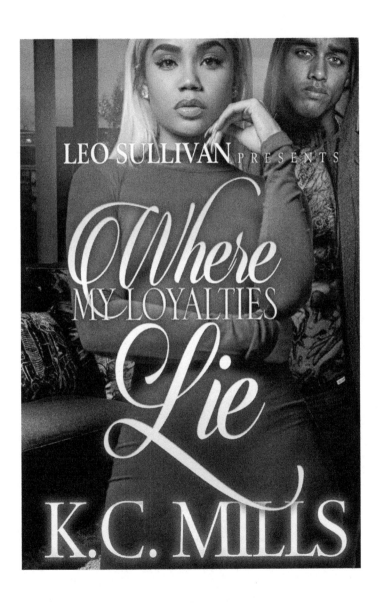

LEO SULLIVAN PRESENTS

Where MY LOYALTIES *Lie*

K.C. MILLS

A Thug's Betrayal

Sativa Outlaw